THE CROSSING

Manjeet Mann

PENGUIN BOOKS

PENGUIN BOOKS

UK | USA | Canada | Ireland | Australia
India | New Zealand | South Africa

Penguin Books is part of the Penguin Random House group of companies
whose addresses can be found at global.penguinrandomhouse.com.

www.penguin.co.uk
www.puffin.co.uk
www.ladybird.co.uk

First published 2021

001

Text copyright © Manjeet Mann, 2021

Text design by Janene Spencer
Printed and bound in Great Britain by Clays Ltd, Elcograf S.p.A.

The authorized representative in the EEA is Penguin Random House Ireland,
Morrison Chambers, 32 Nassau Street, Dublin D02 YH68

A CIP catalogue record for this book is available from the British Library

ISBN: 978-0-241-41144-5

All correspondence to:
Penguin Books
Penguin Random House Children's
One Embassy Gardens, 8 Viaduct Gardens, London SW11 7BW

For the millions of Sammys

366 days before

Everyone is crying but me.
Seven days since she passed.
Seven days, eleven hours, forty-three minutes and sixteen seconds.
Counting the days, hours, minutes,
to stop myself from drowning.

Everyone is crying but me.
Dad squeezes my shoulder.
Be brave, Nat.
I walk towards the front of the church.
Seven days, eleven hours, fifty-three minutes and
nine, ten, eleven, twelve . . .

Everyone is crying but me.
I'm trying to remember how to breathe,
my desert-dry mouth,
hands trembling,
I swallow sand.
It feels like an eternity before I find my   voice.

Everyone is crying but me.
Tears stream down Dad's face –
he's given up wiping them away.
His voice   c   r   a   c   k   s
as he reminds everyone of who she was.
Katherine. Kate . . . Kitty . . .
          her laugh   joy for life   mermaid
                    wonderful mother   beautiful wife . . .
                activist   big heart . . .

my mum.

Everyone is crying.
Everyone,
even **me**.

Me and Mama have lain here on
the cold floor for hours
or seconds.

It's hard
to know
anything
right now.

I lie next to Baba,
his warm hands
turned cold.

I want more than anything
to breathe life back into him.

Baba was fearless
in a country ruled by fear.
I wish I was like you,
I would say.
My son the stargazer,
he would say.
You are perfect just as you are.

Mama moves in waves,
her body undulating,
a crash of howls.

I am a rock.
Unresponsive
to her swells of emotion,
as she beats her chest
and folds into
half the woman she was.

His blood seeps
into my shirt,
staining my skin.

I breathe into the
            holes
                  in
      his
                  chest.

Our salty tears
mix with
his iron blood,
which soaks into
our skin,
our hair,
our guilt,
that we live
and he

doesn't.

Mama looks at me.
In this moment
she is still
and serious.

I can't hide you forever, Samuel.
It is time.
*They will come for you **next**.*

336 days before

I should have taken more videos of her.
I should have recorded every moment,
caught every breath,
savoured every laugh.

I touch the screen,
wanting to grab hold of her –
to reach through my phone and

pull
          her

out.

I wish she was still here, Dad.

I know, love, I know.

Dad's desperate to keep it together,
but he's b r o k e n,
w e   a l l   a r e.

We've kept our distance
these past few months,
keeping our sharp edges to

ourselves.

Getting too close
could cause a puncture
and then we'll see it.
The emptiness.
The grief.
It'll leak out,
or pull us in.

Either way,
there'll be no
escaping
it.

My heart shifts a little,
knowing we'll
never
be the same.

Knowing we won't ever
fit
like before.

Mum was like
winter socks.
She knew how to keep you warm.
She knew how to hold you.

Dad's like fingerless gloves.
He tries, but he doesn't quite
reach your edges –
the important bits –
the bits that really matter.

'Watch this, Nat! Watch me!'
We stare at the screen as Mum
cartwheels straight into the sea
and then emerges, coughing
and laughing,
trying to catch her breath.

That laugh, Ryan says, smiling,
and he's right.

Mum was small,
but she was a powerhouse.
Big laugh.
Big smile.

Big heart.

Ryan slides his finger across the screen
so we can watch the scene play out
again   and   again   and   again.

She was so passionate, wasn't she, Dad?
Like about everything.

She was, Nat, he says. She cared too much, your mum.

You know what she'd say to that, don't you?

What, Nat?

*There's no such thing. You can't care **too much**.*

Too much *time has passed.*
        I trace Baba's face on the screen with my fingertips.
        I memorize his voice.
Eritrea is a country traumatized by war.
        I want to feel his skin.
This once free country is a military prison.
        I whisper his words.
The world's biggest prison.
        I pause the recording.
        I stroke the face on the screen,
        wishing it was skin.
        I press play and the recording restarts.
        I wonder if this video
        is the reason
        he's no longer here.
First the Italians.
        I study Baba's face.
Then the British.
        I watch how he uses his hands.
Then came Ethiopia . . .

I mimic his posture.
Years of war . . .

Baba is animated.
He gestures wildly with his hands,
his eyes bright,
his speech slow,
picking up pace
as he captivates his audience.

I stare at my reflection in the mirror.
I look into my eyes.
I examine my body.
I study my breath,
desperate to see him
in them,
in me.

> *There are many ways to be brave, Sammy.*
> *Most are small, simple acts of courage.*
> *You will find yours.*

Baba's courage
was in his words.

> *Never be afraid to speak up for what is right.*

> *It's too hard, Baba. I feel hopeless.*

> *It's never hopeless, Sammy.*
> *Never. You know why?*

> *Why?*

> *Because no matter how dark it gets*
> *there are still stars in the sky.*

He lived by these words.
Even after Black Tuesday –
the eighteenth of September 2001.

The day seven independent
national newspapers were banned.

The day the Eritrean press
died
and a fully militarized country was
born.

Baba mourned this day
every year.

> *Eritrea, our beautiful country,*
> *has descended into the abyss, Sammy.*
> *It is my job to tell people the truth.*

> *But aren't you scared, Baba?*

> *We have to face our fears if we are to be free, Sammy.*

Mama tells me
he showed no weakness
when the soldiers came for him.
He looked them
straight in the eye
as they
brought
him
down.

I'm not brave, Baba,
You were brave.
Why aren't I?

Why aren't I more like her, Dad?

You are, Nat. You're the spitting image of her.

She had a big heart.

Yours ain't so small.

I feel like my chest has been stamped on.
When's it gonna stop hurting?
Dad?
Dad?

You want the truth?

Always.

Dunno if it does, Nat. I dunno if it ever **does**.

Does the pain ever stop, Mama?

One day . . . it will get easier.

Baba was the sun.

And he still shines.

Nothing lives without the sun.

Why are you talking this way, Sammy?

I am nothing without you both.

You are more . . .

I am dust. Nothing but dust.

Yes you are, Sammy.
Stardust.
*You are the most precious gift of **all**.*

318 days before

My alarm rings at seven thirty.
I've been awake since five.
Habit.

> Rise and shine, Nat! Come on, let's get our feet wet,
> my little scholarship superstar!
>
> You're so embarrassing, Mum!
>
> I'm proud, is all – aren't I allowed to be proud?
> My Nat's gonna be a pro swimmer!
>
> You don't know that.
>
> I do and I'm gonna shout it from the top of Dover Castle!

I hear her voice
in my head
every morning.
But, nah.
Some things died along with her,
and swimming
was one of them.

I peel my body out of bed,
drag myself into the bathroom,
splash cold water on my face.
My skin tightens and tingles.
I look at my reflection in the mirror
and take a deep breath –
try and slow my heart down,
feeling nervous about the day ahead,
mixing with the world again.

**Feels like
I've been hiding
in this house
forever.**

Feels like
I've been hiding
in this house
forever.

Confined to the walls
of my home.
Witnessing the rainbow
of sunrise and sunset
through gaps in the curtains,
stargazing secretly
when all the lights are out.

In the first few weeks
I was cocky –
I thought I'd escaped military camp.
Then came the conscription notices
one
after
the
other.

Then came the soldiers,
threatening Mama,
searching the house.

I hid in the cellar,
breath held,
frozen,
hearing Mama scream,
hearing her pleading,
He left! He's not here! Please!

I am seventeen.
Seventeen and in hiding
for forty-eight
days and nights.

Hiding and waiting.
Waiting for money
from a cousin in America
and an uncle in the UK.

Thousands of pounds.
Enough to get me to Europe,
and fake papers from my best friend, Tesfay.

Tesfay, who knows someone,
who knows someone,
who knows someone.

If you pay enough,
there is always
someone
who knows
someone.

Someone *needs to clean this house,*
Ryan! Ryan!
You live here an' all and I'm always doing it.
It's not fair!

I walk into his room,
pick up his clothes
and throw them at him.
He stirs a little
then turns over.
He'll be like that
all
day.

Since the funeral
the whole house has gone to shit.
Dishes, dirt, laundry, takeaway boxes
littering every surface.

Sunlight streams through the window
revealing the true state
of Dad's room.
Clothes all over the floor,
his work boots and hi-vis
making friends with dishes
and pizza boxes
he's brought up to bed.
A stack of old photos spill out
from under his pillow.

Mum and Dad on their wedding day.
Mum on the beach in Hastings.
Mum sticking out her tongue.
Mum at the local pool with me and Ryan.
Mum and Dad in front of the Eiffel Tower.

There are loads more.
I want to curl up with them,
forget school,
forget life having to   carry   on.

I leave the photos
where I found them
and the bed as it is.

I sit in the kitchen,
eating dry cereal
straight from the box.

I wash three spoons
and three bowls.
Just enough to   **keep   going**.

Keep going, *Sammy*.
I must keep going.
I repeat this over and over
to stop myself from losing my mind.
The waiting is over.
I leave tonight.
The fear of going replaced
with the fear of staying
every day.

I hear Mama making breakfast,
and remember how I would patiently wait
at the kitchen table
for some kitcha fit-fit,
my favourite breakfast.
Bread mixed with
spiced butter and berbere spices,
served with a dollop,
or in my case
lashings, of yoghurt.

Baba sitting in his chair,
drinking thick black coffee.
Take it easy – you'll be eating soon enough.
But I couldn't help it –
the aroma of the spices
drove my stomach crazy.

I remember how I would brush
and rinse my teeth twice afterwards!
I wanted to smell good for my sweet Mariam.
Just in case we might speak.
A year trying to pluck up the courage
to talk to her
and then finally
                    it
                        happened.

It's now or never, Sammy.
School is over – if you don't talk to her now,
you never will.

Tesfay, my wingman,
urging me to make my move.

Seriously, Sammy, say hi, do something.
I can't hear about your heartache any more!

I take a deep breath and
walk towards her.
I look back at Tesfay,
who gives me a thumbs up,
and continue what feels like
the longest walk of my life.
I stand opposite her.

Hi, Mariam, I say too quietly.
Hi, Mariam, I say again,
this time my voice jumping two octaves.
I clear my throat.
Hi, Mariam.

She smiles.
She SMILES
and time stops.
S   a   m   m   y.
I watch her mouth
form shapes that
say my name.
The world continues in slow motion
as I study her lips.

I feel a sharp
nudge in my ribs.

Close your mouth, Tesfay whispers.

Sammy, she says again,
did you want something?

I am lost for words.

What my friend is trying to say, says Tesfay,
is that he would like to take you for some gelato,
if you're free?

Oh, she says, looking surprised,
her gaggle of girlfriends giggling behind her.

My face burns with embarrassment.
What was I thinking?
This is Mariam,
the most beautiful girl in school.
What would she see in me?

You can tell your friend I say OK.

Sitting across from one another in the crowded cafe,
it's like we're the only two people in there.
I can't eat,
my gelato turning into a pool of liquid in the bowl.
You don't have to be so nervous, she says.
I don't bite.

On the way home
my fingers brush against hers as we walk.
It's electric.
You can hold my hand, she says.
I take it and
my heart skips a beat.

We stand outside her house.
Thank you for joining me, I say.

You're welcome. Thank you for the gelato.

We are standing so close,
I can smell the strawberry gelato on her breath.
It's OK. You can kiss me, she says,
closing her eyes and leaning forward.

I can still taste it.

She was taken to Sawa a few days later
on the last day of school, along with
thirty others, while Tesfay and I
hid like dogs.

It was the start and end of
something beautiful.
Now, like most things,
it's too **late**.

Late *for school*,
I think, looking at the clock,
not moving,
staring into nothingness.
Come on, Nat, get your coat on,
I tell myself, watching the minutes   tick   by.

I continue sipping
cold, bitter coffee.
Everything tastes
bitter these days.
I can't remember
the last time
something tasted
good.

A HERD OF MIGRANTS
SWARM DOVER BEACHES

I see the headline from across the kitchen table,
can't be bothered to pick it up and read the full story.

The same one
almost
every
day.

Mum was a refugee support worker.
If she was here, she'd be helping.
She'd come home crying some nights,
finding it hard to separate herself,
her heart was that big.

Come on, you two, give your mum a big hug.

Ugh, that's enough, Mum.
Ryan wipes his cheek with his sleeve.

You don't mind, do you, Natty?

Nope!

*I don't know what I'd do
if anything happened to this family.*

Ow, Mum, you're squeezing me too tight.

*Oops, sorry, Natty. I just love you so much.
I want to squish you down and put you in my pocket.*

Can't say I ever gave her job much thought.
It all seemed so distant somehow.
It never really   connected.

I was mostly annoyed
by the long hours she'd work.
Other families,
other children
getting more of her
than me.

I wipe away tears
on my school shirt,
forgetting I'm wearing mascara.
I look at the black smudges on my sleeve,
and take another sip of bitterness.
I don't have it in me to think.
I don't have it in me to care.

My phone beeps.
Mel: There's late and then there's late, babe.
       Where are you?

I look at the clock.
I have no intention
of leaving any time soon.
       10 mins. Soz
I lie.

I lie to Tesfay.
I tell him I'm excited.
I tell him I'm feeling brave.

He has come with the fake papers.
The final piece of the jigsaw.
The day I've been
dreading and dreaming of
has arrived.

We're out of here, Sammy!
We finally have our ticket out of here!

Tesfay is small for eighteen –
he just about comes up to my shoulder,
with a scrawny frame to match.
But Tesfay is mighty.
We've known each other
all our lives.

Tesfay means 'hope'
and on this journey
he'll be just that.
I couldn't do it without him.
He's the only person,
apart from Mama, I've seen
this past month.

This past month
things between me and Ryan
have gone from bad to worse.
He's . . . different.
Sleeping all day,
out all night,
drinking,
smoking weed
and
getting inked.
The latest –
a rose –
covering half his arm.

Ryan . . . Ryan . . . RYAN!

What? he mumbles
from deep under
the duvet.

Dad left some money for the shopping – can you do it?
Ryan?
Ry?

Yeah! Get lost! he snaps.

It's like he's had a personality transplant.
Dad says he's rebelling and
it's normal after what we've been through.
I asked him why I'm not rebelling

and he said, *You're sixteen. There's still time.*

I slam Ryan's bedroom door,
stomp down the stairs,
grab my coat and rucksack
and notice a purple cardigan
hung up
behind
Dad's parka.

I thought he'd got rid of everything.
He had a clear-out
two weeks after the funeral.
Like getting rid of her stuff
was all we needed to   move on.

> *She would have hated us holding on to them, Nat.*
> *You know what she'd say,*
> *'No point keeping my old stuff when there are others*
> *who are more in need.'*
> *Trust me, this is what she would have wanted.*

But it wasn't what I wanted.
I want to see her in every room.
I want to keep remembering.

I take her cardigan off the hook,
hold the sleeve
against my cheek.
It's soft – like her.
Warm – like her.
The scent of her perfume –
lingering, sweet – like her.

I put it on.
It's not school colours
but I don't care.
I wrap her round me.
I need you with me today,

I whisper to no one.

I think of Ryan upstairs
and slam the front door extra hard
on the way out.

On the way out of Asmara
we have to be clever,
stay hidden in the shadows.

Tesfay is calmer now.
His face is serious.
He speaks quietly.

I listen,
my heart racing,
knowing I have to leave,
yet wishing this day would
never come,
paralysed by my fear
of the journey,

knowing the dangers,
knowing our fate if we don't make it,
knowing our fate if we stay,
knowing what's at stake.

Tesfay has a map
with red lines drawn across it,
plotting our journey
all the way to the UK.

It will take two weeks maximum, he says
and then punches the air with his fist.

To Europe! he says.

To Europe, I say,
desperate to match
his enthusiasm,
but

**there's a lump
the size of the moon
in my throat
taking up space
where courage
should be.**

**There's a lump
the size of the moon
in my throat
taking up space
where courage
should be**
and my heart's
beating faster
than it should.

Just when I think of
turning back,
running back,
I see Mel.

Mel!
I fall into her arms,
she kisses me on the mouth,
and just for a moment
everything slows down.

Everything slows down.
The mood has changed.
The two of us sit in silence,
thinking,

not speaking
of the dangers
that lie ahead.

Which
one
will
end
us?

Caught at a checkpoint
before leaving Asmara,
and thrown into prison
or executed?
Or captured later on,
tortured,
sold into slavery
or murdered
if a ransom isn't paid?

Do you want to end up like your sister Sophia
in Sawa training camp?

Sophia,
who we haven't
heard from
in a year.
Still not knowing
whether we can
mourn for her.

We have nothing to lose, Sammy.
Live as slaves in Eritrea
or risk death and slavery if we leave.
But, if we make it . . .

Exactly, if we make it . . .

Yes. If we make it, we're free.
Free! You can study your stars;
I can design glass skyscrapers!
We can live the life we always dreamed of.

But I can't help how I . . .
I keep getting this . . . like rocks on my chest . . .
and I . . . I . . .

I drop my head into my hands.
Tesfay puts his arm round my shoulder.
He squeezes me into him.

We've dreamed of this day for so long.

I know, I say.
I know.

Look, Tesfay, a plane!

Hey! Hey!
Tesfay waves his arms at the passing plane.
My friend Sammy and I want to escape from here.
Take us with you!

Those planes
like shooting stars.

So why do I feel
like I'm losing my mind?
I just want everything to stop.

I just want everything to stop, I sob.
Mel's warm and she smells like spring.
Like, if time moves too quick, I'll forget Mum.

I feel unbalanced.

Mel takes my face in her hands
and kisses each eyelid.
She calls them angel kisses.

You won't, she says.

It feels like I already have. It's almost two months –
what's it gonna be like in another two months?
What's it gonna be like in two years?

We don't have to go in today if you're not feeling up to it.
We can go back to mine. Hang out.

It's the first day back from summer break, Mel. We can't.

Mel and I are opposites.
I like rules.
Mel's happy to break them.

I always thought
she was too good for me.
Too posh. Too rich.
What would she ever see in me?
        I'm the quiet girl from the estate
        just wanting to blend in.
Mel's sparky,
out and proud and loud.
        I just want to be invisible.
Mel wants to be seen. A wannabe social-media influencer,
she's all about being *ahead of the curve* –
        I'm fine being behind it.
Mel wants to travel.
        I can't see myself leaving Dover.

Mum used to say
I was the yin to Mel's yang.
We balance each other out.

But I'm frightened

I won't be able to keep up
and she'll soon realize
I'm not good **enough**.

Enough, Sammy. Shh.

I'm sorry, Tesfay. I'm sorry I'm such a coward.

Are you kidding? I'm so frightened I've had stomach ache for months.

What? You're always so . . .

Strong? Confident? Fearless . . .?

Well . . . yes.

You have to fake it till you make it.
And we will make it, Sammy. We will.

I can't seem to let go of the dangers
as easily as Tesfay.

There are so many before
we even cross the border, before
we survive the desert, before
we risk our lives on
the boats.

The boats.
Everyone's talking about
the boats.

The boats
the boats
the boats.

I look at Fazel.

The boy who came to our school last year.
The boy who came on a boat.
The boy who never makes eye contact.
The boy who says nothing when a pen is thrown at his head.
The boy who lost everything.
The boy who lost **everyone**.

Everyone   knows these dangers.
Everyone   knows the score.
Everyone   is risking their life.
Everyone   knows they could die.
Everyone   would rather die than stay.

Rather die   than stay.
Risk
their
life   **to live**.

                    ***To live** like that in a war zone*
                    or a place with no human rights.
                    Imagine, Nat.
                    Just imagine leaving everything behind
                    and losing everyone
                    you ever loved.

Mum's
voice
chimes
in
my
head.

Kevin
       pushes
              Fazel

                his
                        chair.

I watch.
I imagine.
I say nothing.

I say nothing
as Mama looks at the fake papers,
and fake military pass.

I see the tears in her eyes.
She turns away again,
trying desperately to
cover the cracks in her voice.
I'll make you something to eat –
you must be hungry.

You must be hungry –
you're stuffing that sandwich down your face
like you haven't seen food before.

I'm starving.
I've only had a handful of cereal this morning.

Slow down! You'll give yourself indigestion.

Whatever, snob.
I open my mouth,
give her an eyeful
of the contents.

Ugh! Gross!

We hide behind the sports hall.
Mel sucks on a cigarette

and then passes it to me.
I take a long drag.

What you thinking? she asks,
taking the cigarette back.

I feel bad for Fazel.

You can't fight everyone's battles, babe.

Maybe you can.
Maybe you should
at least try, anyway.

*That's your mum **talking**.*

Talking to Mama is
like getting
blood
from
a
stone.

She's silent,
staring at her food,
moving it round her plate.

We sit at the table,
in a room that once vibrated with music,
where Sophia and I would secretly watch
Baba and Mama dancing after dinner,
long after they'd put us to bed.

I smile at the memory.
Mama looks at me.
What? she asks.

of you and Baba and
loved watching you dance.
were asleep,
hind the sofa and watch.

She smile...
Oh, we knew,
and I think I see
a tiny flicker of light
in her eyes.

Mama, this is our last day.
Her smile fades and
she shakes her head
like she's bitten
into something rotten.

It's not the last.
Don't say last.
Never say last.

She picks up her glass
without having taken a sip
and stands over the sink.

My heart can't take losing another child.
Do you understand, Sammy?
You must be brave, Sammy.
*You must **be brave**.*

Be brave, *Nat.*
Don't be a sheep. You step up for those who can't
and use what you've got to do something good.

I take another drag of Mel's cigarette,
try and forget Mum's words,
try and hide what I've become
behind a cloud of smoke.

Mel crouches behind the bins
and writes up two notes,
and forges two signatures,
to get us out of PE.

I stare at my reflection
in the sports-hall window.
I had a swimming scholarship.
I showed promise.
Shit grades but at least I could swim.
Didn't bother applying this year.
Mum filled out the form,
but I couldn't.
I had no interest.
Swimming can fuck right off,
I think, and take another drag.

Who am I?
This smoking,
PE-dodging girl
hiding behind the dustbins.

Hiding behind the dustbins,
Tesfay and I avoided
Sawa military camp.

We saw the military bus
and the men with their rifles
outside our school
and made a

        run

                for

                    it.

We hid behind the large school bins,
holding our shirts over our noses,
trying to cover the smell and
stop ourselves from seeing

our lunch in reverse.

I peeked through a crack in the metal
and saw all the kids from our year –
my school friends,
my beautiful Mariam –
being hauled on to the bus,
the bus for Sawa training camp
and years of abuse and torture.

We waited till it drove away,
and it was way after dark
before we were brave enough
to run home.

I hold Mama tight.
I feel her resist.

Sammy, please, you're not making this easy.

I tighten my hold and
sink into her shoulder.
I wish nothing had to change.

I wish nothing had to change.
I really do. But this is just how it is.

We're sitting round the kitchen table.
Dad holds a piece of paper in his hand
that's turned our world upside down.

Where are we gonna live, Dad? I ask.

I dunno, love. We'll find somewhere.

Ryan sits with his arms folded,
silent,

like his mouth's been stitched up.

*But we've been on the council list for ages
and nothing's come up.*

I know, Nat. I know.

*The landlord can't do this, can he, Dad?
He can't just throw us out?*
My voice shakes as
I try and hold back tears.

Ryan pushes his plate   across the table,
gets up,
knocks his
                chair
                        down.

Ryan! Calm down!

No, Dad. It's bullshit!

He leaves,
slamming the door behind him.
The vibrations
cause a photo of Mum
to fall from the wall.

**The glass breaks into
three   separate   pieces.**

**The glass breaks into
three   separate   pieces.**
Mama stands over the sink, crying.

*I'll make it to Europe.
I promise, Mama.*

She
collapses
to
her
knees.

I'm sorry, Sammy.
I'm sorry.

I'm sorry, *Nat. I'm trying to do my best here. I really am.*

I know, Dad.

Your mum was always better at this sort of stuff,
especially with Ryan.

It's no secret Ryan and I
were closer to Mum.
She just knew
how to hold your heart,
make you feel
whole again.

Since she died
Dad can't even
look at me.

I'm heading to bed, Nat. Don't worry about clearing up.
You must have homework. Go on, this can wait. **I'm tired**.

I'm tired of crying, Sammy.
She's hunched over.
Her voice splits
and pain spills out.

Samuel, she says. *Don't say goodbye.*

What do you mean?

When you leave. Don't say goodbye.
I can't bear to say goodbye.

Mama . . .

I'm going to bed, Sammy.
It's late.

It's late.
I can't sleep.
I get out of bed
and grab a bag full of clothes
hidden at the back of my wardrobe.

A bag Dad told me
to take to the charity shop,
but I couldn't
bring myself
to part with them.

Her yellow leather gloves,
her pink knitted scarf,
her red woolly hat,
her orange fleece jumper.
All the things she wore after a swim
still carrying her scent.

I add this morning's
purple cardigan to the stash.
I wear it all.
I stare down at myself, smiling
at the mishmash of colours.

Nutritionists say eat the rainbow to keep your heart healthy.
I say wear the rainbow to keep your mind smiling.
Don't laugh at me, it's true!

Your clothes match your personality, Nat.
You can tell a lot about a person
by the colours they wear.
Keep them bright, I say.

Fifty-five days,
eight hours,
forty-seven minutes
and twelve seconds.

It'll take time.
That's what everyone says.
One day at a time.
It gets easier.
You'll get over it.

I don't want to get over it.
I don't want to forget her.

I don't want to forget her.
My mama.
Be brave.
The words
throw themselves
round my head.

You have to face your fears if you're to be free.

I see Baba's face.
Well, Baba, I'm not fighting like you.
I hid and now I'll run.

I take his watch
out of my desk drawer
and put it on.
It's time.

I pack light –
I can't look suspicious –
I'm a soldier on leave for
one night only.

I have a fake military pass,
photos, and
one thousand dollars
sewn into my clothes.

I stare at my reflection.
I take a deep breath
and really look at myself in the mirror . . .

I stare at my reflection.
I take a deep breath
and really look at myself in the mirror . . .

the photo
from the broken frame
in my hand.

I look at her
and
back at myself.

You're the spitting image of her, Nat.

And I wonder
if that's why
Dad can't stand
to look at me.

I take out her bright red
swimming costume and swim cap
from my drawer.
She was going to make it across the Channel in these.
A wave of anger and sadness

washes over me as I stuff them
into the bag at the back of the wardrobe
with the rest of her clothes.

I creep down the stairs
and round the house.
It's a habit I've formed,
these midnight walks,
remembering her
in every room.

In every room
I see my family.

Sophia sitting at the kitchen table, doing her homework.
Mama and Baba dancing in the lounge.
Music fills my ears and my heart swells
as I feel the love in every corner of this house.
I breathe in all the **memories**.

Memories in every room.
Making cupcakes in the kitchen when we were little.
Movie nights, snuggling up in the lounge under a big blanket.
Sitting on the stairs with Ryan after hearing about Mum's diagnosis.
Ryan didn't talk so much after that.

Mum in the lounge,
her hospital bed
over where the telly is now.

I still feel her in there.
I can't go in –
close the door instead.

And now we have to leave
cos some bastard landlord is
kicking us out.

I decide to stay up and clean.
It's 2 a.m. before I'm
finished **in the kitchen**.

In the kitchen
there's a bag.
Inside,
enough food for a day or so.
Dried fruit, bread, water and nuts.
I'm about to leave when
Mama grabs me.

Sammy! Sammy, you haven't gone.
Oh, thank God.

Mama.

We hold each other
for the longest time.
She cups my face
in her hands.

Whatever happens, Sammy,
do not forget
how to love,
your worth,
who you are,
how to feel.
Keep checking,
because when you see awful sights –
and you will –
these are the things that are easy to forget.

I won't, Mama.

I take one more look at my home.
I breathe in my mother,

my sister, my father,
and step out into
the **night**.

317 days before

Dreaming
of a person
who's passed
is beautiful.

> My little water baby, come on –
> let's swim all our troubles away!

> We dive in,
> holding hands,
> dancing under the waves.

> The water heals, Nat.
> Do you feel it?
> Do you?

> Floating on our backs,
> watching the clouds,
> music comes from somewhere

> and we dive
> and race
> and play.

Dreaming
of a person
who's passed
is beautiful.

It's only when you wake
you have to mourn
all over
again.

Again, Tesfay demands.
I repeat our story.

We're brothers.
We're going to meet our aunt.
She lives outside Asmara.
We're staying for the weekend.

Good. Now stop looking so guilty, he says.
We walk into the night,
starting a journey
we have up until now only
heard about.
There are police checkpoints
at every turn.

How are we going make it past all these checkpoints?
I whisper into Tesfay's ear.

Be cool, he whispers back.
There's a hard edge
to his voice.
I swallow
my fear.

We navigate the first two
in the hot, sticky heat
in the dead of night
without any trouble.

The sounds of traffic,
horns and
people shouting
make me jump
at every turn.

The streets seem to close in on me.
The air feels too thick to breathe.

I'm drowning in
fear and the smell of death
on every corner we turn.

Tesfay and I
stay close together
as we arrive at the final checkpoint.

The guard –
a boy our age –
looks at us
for too long.

Tesfay is cool.
He cracks a joke.
The boy doesn't laugh.
I can feel the beads of sweat
rolling down my temples.

Only when we're sitting on the bus
do I realize I've been holding
my breath.

I'm a coward compared to Tesfay.
Tesfay who is half my size
with double the courage.

We're walking into death, Tesfay.

We die if we stay,
we die if we get caught,
we might die in the Sahara,
we might die in the sea,
but one thing is certain:
if we escape –
we live.
We live, Sammy.
Do you hear me?

The chance to live
is worth dying for.

The chance to live
is worth dying for.
That's what Mum said to Dad
when he told her there was no way
she could swim the Channel
in her condition.

> *For God's sake, Pete, I need something to take my mind*
> *off being a sick person! It'll be healing, Pete. I feel it in my bones,*
> *in my cells. There's nothing like being in the water. You'll see.*

> *I'll swim with her. I'll help her train. She won't be alone, Dad.*

> *You'd really do that for me, Nat?*

> *Yeah, course.*

> *Thank you, Natty.*

> *Oh, don't cry, Mum.*

> *I can't help it. This chemo's got me puking,*
> *pissing and blubbering all over the shop!*

But she was wrong.
It didn't heal her.
It didn't heal her at **all**.

All *you need to do is follow my lead.*
Actually –
Tesfay pauses for a moment –
maybe it's better if you leave the talking to me.

The bus starts to pull out of the station.

I sit back and look at the city
I'm leaving behind.

> *The city of Italian gods.*
> *Or so they like to think.*

> *What do you mean, Baba?*

> *They took us over, Sammy,*
> *and built all their churches,*
> *but when we flee war and oppression,*
> *they won't accept us in their country.*
> *To them we are vermin.*

This is the start of our journey.
Eritrea to the UK.
Over five thousand kilometres to
paradise.
Over five thousand kilometres to a new
home.

Home is the last place
I wanna be.
We sit in separate rooms.
Ryan in the living room, playing computer games.
Dad in the kitchen, looking through bills.
I stay in my bedroom,
the distance between us growing each day.

Dad doesn't look at us.
Ryan doesn't talk.
I don't ask questions.

I close my eyes
and think of Mum,
wishing we'd had more **time**.

Time to put our plan into action, Tesfay says.
Don't look so guilty.
He nudges me in the ribs.
Give me your ticket and
pretend to be asleep or
you'll give us away, he whispers.

I slump down in my seat,
pull my cap over my face
and fold my arms,
trying to look relaxed.

I sense the ticket inspector looming over us.
I want to look, but dare not open my eyes,
not even a tiny bit.

He prods me.
It takes all my effort not to flinch.
Like an animal,
I play dead.

He's asleep, I hear Tesfay lie.
We've had a very tiring week in training.
We're on our way to visit our aunt in the next village,
just for the weekend.

Passes, I hear the man say.
Tesfay reaches into my jacket pocket.
My heart pounds.

Silence.

Sweat
pours
down
my
back.

Enjoy your weekend.

We will, and you,
Tesfay says politely.
I hear the inspector laugh and walk away.

I open my right eye,
just a little.
I see Tesfay in my peripheral vision.
He nudges me in the ribs again and winks.

Now you can relax.

I am relaxed, I say.

You forget how long I've known you.
I know how you're feeling.

I know how you're feeling, Mr Lennon.

*No you don't. I don't think you know how I'm feeling at all.
How can you? I put my name on that council list months ago
and now we're being evicted and you haven't done
a sodding thing about it.*

You're three months behind with the rent.

Three months, Dad?
You didn't tell me you were three months behind.

*The landlord put the rent up by four hundred quid!
Four hundred fucking quid a month!*

Mind your language, please, Mr Lennon.

*I'll mind my language when you tell me how he's allowed
to do that! No notice. Just four hundred extra quid a month.
Just like that!*

49

He's perfectly within his rights to do that.

How is that fair! I've got kids. They've not long lost their mum . . .

I understand all that, Mr Lennon . . .

No you don't! How can you have any idea . . .

Calm down, Mr Lennon, or I'll have to call security . . .

Please don't do that.
It's all right, Dad . . .
I hold his hand.
It's all right, **I whisper**.

I whisper my goodbyes to the coffee shops,
the hours spent chatting with friends
over cappuccinos.
The art deco theatre.
The Cinema Impero.
The gelato cafe
I took Mariam to
on our first
and last date.
I can barely
hold back tears,
my throat choked.
I'm leaving **my home**.

My home. It's my home!
You understand that, don't you?

Yes, I understand, Mr Lennon. I've told you, I'm doing all I
can to get you into another place.
But you have to understand that our budgets
have been cut.

*Look . . . There might be the possibility of a one-bed flat.
Shared bathroom, but you'll have your own kitchenette and
separate lounge which can be used as a second bedroom.*

*Shared bathroom? No way – I've got a teenage daughter and
a teenage son. We need three bedrooms.*

*Your son's eighteen and I'm right in thinking he's not
in education?*

Yeah . . .

*I can give you a list of private rentals for your son.
My priority is you and your daughter.*

*He can't afford a private rental, he's on a zero-hours contract –
he barely gets anything. Anyway, I ain't having him living on his
own, no way. For God's sake, are you even listening?*

Mr Lennon, I'll not warn you again.

Dad, please keep calm.

*We have over seven thousand people on the waiting list
and less than one thousand places come up for rent
every year. I'm trying my best for you. Really I am.
Look . . . there's a meeting in Orchid House in a few
days' time. Councillor Emery will be there talking about
the new Prospect Homes development. It might be worth
going along . . . Here, take a leaflet.*

*This can't be happening.
Honest to God, just tell me what I need to do
to get a place for me and my kids.
What's gonna make us a priority?
Just tell me and I'll do it.
Please.
Please.
Please.
I feel like I'm in **a nightmare**.*

A nightmare.

                    I am a body
                        scorched
                    by the sun.

                    A mouth
                        full of
                        sand.

                    I am a body
                        drowned
                    by the sea.

                    Eyes taken,
                        bloated,
                        sinking

                        sinking
                        sinking
                        sinking.

Mama! I shout out,
waking with a jolt,
sweat pouring from my body.

Are you OK?
Tesfay says, looking over at me.
I nod.
**My mouth dry,
unable to form words.**

**My mouth dry,
unable to form words.**
Dad and I walk in silence.
Finally, I muster the courage to ask him . . . .

We're going to be all right, aren't we?

I'll make sure we are.

We're going to be all right, aren't we?

I'll make sure we are, Sammy.

We drive the whole night.
For fear of another nightmare,
I don't sleep.
Wiping dirt from the window
and looking for stars instead.

It makes me feel so small looking up at the night sky, Baba.

Why small? It should make you feel powerful.

How so?

Do you know all the events that had to happen to create this planet?
All the events that had to take place to create life?
It's extraordinary, Sammy. We're a mathematical anomaly.
We're a rarity. Once you realize the statistical odds of our existence,
when you look up there, it shouldn't make you feel small, it should remind you
of all the possibilities that exist in space,
all the possibilities that exist in us.

Sunrise paints a rainbow of reds
across the sky
as we arrive in Teseney
near the Sudanese border.

This is where
we have to
tread carefully.

This is where
we have to
find a smuggler

to take us over
the border
on the other side of the mountains.

Tesfay and I wait by the bus station.
Waiting for too long could get us
killed right here,
right now

> or
> caught,
> sent back
> and executed
> for deserting.

Our stomachs grumble with hunger as
we try to make the little food we have
last as long as possible.
We share a handful of nuts and raisins,
watching women in headscarves
and men in cream jalabiyas
getting on and off buses.

Chickens, goats and children
mingle in the chaos.
We stay in the shadows
as the magic of sunrise disappears
and turns into scorching heat.

I thank God I'm here with Tesfay,
who never loses faith,
but no matter how hard we try
we can't tell the people smugglers
apart from the other traders.

We've waited nearly the entire day,
and just when I think we're out of luck
I notice a large man looking in our direction.

He walks over to us.
His jalabiya billowing in the breeze
makes him look double the size
and twice as frightening.
You want to get over the border?
he says in a hushed tone.

Yes, we say,
having no idea whether we can
trust him or not.

Come with me, he says.
We follow him through the busy streets
to a house
with a room
behind a room.

No windows,
no light.
A dirt floor
and three other boys.

We wait.

We wait
behind the sports hall,
eating our sandwiches.
Corned beef for me –
Mel's got some
gourmet-supermarket-finest creation
with houmous and
roasted peppers.

How did it go with the housing officer?

Shit.

Sorry.

Not your fault.

She offers me an olive.

No thanks.

She keeps offering them.
I'm gonna make you an olive person if it's the last thing I do.

And I'll make you a corned-beef person if it's the last thing I do.

She pretends she's gonna puke.

You're such a snob, I half joke.

The last bell rings.
I stuff the rest of my sandwich into my mouth
and leg it to registration.

When we get there,
everyone's sniggering.
It's only when we take our seats
that we notice Kevin Smith has drawn
a cartoon picture on the whiteboard
of a boatful of refugees, with a caption saying,
Fazel's missing family

I look over at Fazel,
who stares at the board,
not blinking.

When Mrs Bates walks in,
she takes one look at the drawing

and then at us.

Who did that?

       Silence.

Detention for the whole class if someone doesn't own up.

       Silence.

No one wants Kevin on their back
for the rest of the school year.

Looks like it's detention then.
And she proceeds to clean the whiteboard,
muttering,
*You should be ashamed. Horrible. Just **horrible**.*

Horrible.
We share the space
with cockroaches
and mosquitoes.
I'm constantly
swiping them away
while Tesfay engages with the
three other Eritrean boys –
Hamid, Petros, Yonas.

Where are you headed? Tesfay asks.

Europe,
they all say
one after the other.

You? Hamid asks.

Same, Tesfay tells them.

UK. Sammy's uncle is there,
and my cousin is too.

All of us running
from the same fate.
All of us wishing
for the same future.

Can this man be trusted? I ask.

I think so, says Yonas,
the oldest of the three.
He's eighteen but looks much older.

Petros is quiet.
He's only fourteen and
escaped from Sawa.
It's common knowledge
they take poorer children
at much younger ages.
They have less choice, it seems.

Hamid is sixteen and the joker.
I'm amazed at how anyone
can keep their spirits up
in a place like this,
but I'm grateful for his humour.

We're quiet again.
Only the hiss of the cockroaches
and the whine of the mosquitoes
providing a soundtrack
to our European dreams.

Hours go by.
I try to rest.
I try to forget.
I close my eyes

and drift
in
        and
out
        of
sleep.

I drift
     I drift
          I drift . . .

Hey, Baba, you're here?

Of course – where else would I be?

You're alive . . .

I'm five,
riding my bike
down our street.

Don't let go, Baba.

I won't, Sammy.

You promise?

I promise!

I'm ten.
I'm flying a kite.

Sophia . . . Sophia!!!!

She's sitting on the grass,
reading a book.

Sophia!!!

She looks up at me and smiles
and suddenly I'm older.
Baba takes my kite and runs into the wind.

Baba! Baba! You're here!
Did you see Sophia?

Yes, I found Sophia.
She's with me now.

And he runs and runs,
and I try to run after him,
but I can't move. I'm trying so hard to run,
but I'm stuck . . . *Baba!*

Sammy. Sammy. Sammy.
Tesfay is shaking me awake.
You were shouting for Sophia, for your Baba.

Sorry, I gasp.

I'm desperate to fall asleep again,
desperate to catch the dream
before it's lost forever.

I drift
        I drift
                I drift.

I drift through the afternoon's lessons.
I think about
the drawing,
the bullying,
my silence.

Promise me you'll always speak up, Nat.
You have to cos no one else will.

It's easy to get people to hate.
I've told you enough stories for you to know,
really know.
Look at me, Nat.
Promise me.

I promise, Mum.

I didn't realize how easy
it would be to **break**.

314 days before

Sometime later the man is back.
I think it's morning,
although
it's hard to tell
in this windowless
room behind a room.

He says our smuggler
wants more money.
It now costs an extra
three hundred dollars
on top of the five hundred
we've already paid.

Eight hundred dollars each.
That is his price
to take us over
the Sudanese border.
With its mines
and soldiers.

Being a smuggler
must be the best job
on the continent –
they make the most money.

We can live or die –
it makes no difference
to them.

Either way,
they'll always
get **paid**.

Paid work. I just need some paid work, please.
I thought you said I could have shifts all week?
Right . . . OK . . . OK . . . Thanks for fucking nothing.

He throws the phone against a wall.

Take it easy, Ryan!

He claws at the kitchen counter,
staring out of the window,
his back pulsing.
What we gonna do, Nat?

You'll get work.
I stand next to him.
It feels awkward.
It never used to.

How can that be allowed to happen? he says
as we watch a family
move into a house on the estate.

That place should be ours.

There's lots of people who need homes, Ry.

Yeah, but they don't give them to the likes of us, do they?

What do you mean?

People born in this country should take priority.

How do you know they're not born here?

Look at them.

We stand staring for a while longer
as the woman and her two small children
move into their new home.

Fuck this day, he says.

My eyes sting with tears.
I think back to the days when we would
search the beach together for driftwood.
How he'd get lost in himself for hours,
carving little figures,
making something beautiful
out of something so ordinary,
leaving them round the house
like little gifts for us to find.

I'm going to bed.
Mind how you close that fucking front door!
He storms upstairs.

I wipe my eyes,
throw my dishes in the sink
and slam the front door
on my way out
over and over again.

Over and over again
the same thoughts
go round my head.

Is anyone scared? I ask.

Of course.
Yonas looks at me.
Of course – I'm terrified.

In two weeks we'll be in the UK, Sammy.
Remember Dawit from school?
His younger brother made it to Germany in ten days.
The UK is only a little further from there.

But there's another sea to cross before the UK, Tesfay.

Don't worry. It's a small one.
I've heard people swim it for fun.
Also there's a tunnel under the water
that will take us straight to the UK.

Tesfay's optimism
is beginning to grate.
He's naïve
and I'm always scared.
This thought angers me
even more.

Whatever you're thinking, Sammy,
cheer up – it might never happen.

Cheer up – it might never happen, says Mel.

It already has and it looks and smells like Ryan.

I know, babe. He's turned into a dickhead. I'm sorry.
She nuzzles her face into my neck.
Let's have fun.
Fancy the beach?

I've not been down to the beach
since mine and Mum's last swim
about a month before she died.
I've been avoiding it,
hibernating at home the whole summer,
even refusing Mel's sea-view mansion.

I'm not gonna chuck you in.
Just let's sit and look.
Remind ourselves of the big world that's out there.
Nothing else.
I promise.

She holds my hand
tight in hers.

Come on. **Trust me**.

Trust me.
We're going to be OK.
We're going to make it.

Tesfay,
staying true to his name.
Giving me hope.

I fear I'm too soft for this journey
and my softness will leave Tesfay
to do more than he needs to.
More than he can with**stand**.

Standing on the beach,
looking out at the ferries
going to France,
I feel
hollow.

You know if you scream at the sea, no one can hear you.

Really? I can't tell if Mel's joking.

You never done it?

No.

It's fun, she says.

I'd look like a weirdo.

No you won't. There's no one else around.
Go on. Give it a go. I dare you.

I'm scared what might come out.

Exactly. Scream out the **fear**.

Fear is a noose
around my neck.
Forget my dreams,
Mama is the only family left.
I could leave this room now
and take the bus back to her.

Let's make a pact, says Yonas.
Let's travel together. Brothers in arms. Look out for one another.
Together we can keep each other safe and, more importantly, company.
Hamid will keep us laughing.
Petros is quiet now, but I know he can tell a good story or two.
I'm the oldest so I'll keep you in check. You know, get you to bed on time, no
mischief, make sure you eat your vegetables!
Tesfay is the positivity man – he'll keep our spirits up – and Sammy here . . .

There's silence and
I'm embarrassed –
all I've shown is fear.
I have nothing to offer.

. . . You are the wise one. You'll guide us to freedom.

Tesfay slaps me on the back and says,
Yes, he will. No one knows the stars better than Sammy.
He's our very own road map.

Excellent, we have our private GPS system! Hamid jokes.

Sure! I say,
grateful to be given a purpose.
I can do that!

It's a deal then? says Yonas.
You know the proverb:
'If you want to go fast, go alone.
If you want to go far, go together.'

Yonas puts his hand out
in the middle of the circle.
Hamid puts his on top,
followed by Tesfay,
then Petros, and finally me.

Together, says Yonas.

Together! we shout
and right then and there
a new family
is **born**.

Born a month early, I was.
Mum used to say I took to swimming so well
because I was trying to swim back to the womb,
make up for the month I lost.

Mel takes my hand.
Let's get a bit closer, she says.

We make our way down
to the water's edge,
my legs shaking
as I remember
the last time
I was here
with Mum.

     Are you sure you wanna do this, Mum?

      Yes, Nat. You coming with me or not?

She walked proudly towards the water,
so thin by then
even her swimming costume was baggy.
Her body frail, but her mind
as tough as old boots.

She was exhausted before she even got started
so I held her as she floated on her back.
It was like holding a baby chick.

Mel and I
look out
towards France.

Ahhhhhhhhhhhhhhhhh!
Mel does a horror-movie-worthy scream.

Try it. Go on.
I won't listen, if that helps.

I nod and Mel walks away.
I close my eyes.

Would you look at the sky, Nat!
Look at how the sun creates a halo round the fluffy clouds.
It's beautiful.
Thanks, Nat.
Thanks for holding me up.

That's OK. You're weightless in the water.

I don't mean just today, Nat.

Something buried
deep inside
begins to stir.

Something I've been
pushing
down
begins to rise.

Ahhhhhhhhhhhhhhhhhhhhhhhhhhhhhh!

The scream comes
from the pit of my stomach,
from the depths of my lungs,
from the soles of my feet.

Ahhhhhhhhhhhhhhhhhhhhhhhhhhhhhh!

I'm on my knees,
crying and screaming.
Throwing fistfuls of pebbles
into the sea.

You didn't heal her.
You didn't heal her!
The one thing you were supposed to do.

I'm scooping up pebbles and
throwing them,
screaming as loud as I can
for as long as I can
until nothing but a
dry, sore whisper can   escape
from **my throat**.

My throat feels like
I've swallowed
sand and grit.

No food or water
for nearly twenty-four hours.

The man tells us
we'll be leaving
as soon as it gets dark.

Cockroaches scuttle
round our feet.
I try and brush them away.

Don't send them in my direction, Tesfay says.

They're everywhere. It makes no difference, says Hamid.
Just make sure they don't get into your ears.

I look at him, confused.

Well, you know they'll lay their eggs
in your brain and after three days they'll
hatch and you'll have cockroaches
spewing out of your eyes and nose and mouth?

What?

Oh yeah, everyone knows that, Petros says.

There's a moment's silence and
then the boys burst out laughing.

I'm sorry, man, but you make it too easy!
Hamid is doubled over, laughing.

Seriously. You need to toughen up, says Yonas.
This is only the beginning.
There's so much worse ahead.
The desert,
the sea,
the bodies.
Children, mothers, fathers who no one will ever read about,
that loved ones will never hear from . . .

I wait for the laughter,
but it doesn't come.

I wait for the laughter,
but it doesn't come.
Screaming at the sea
has left me exhausted.

Is this how I'm always going to feel, Mel?
Empty?

For a while.
She puts her hand in mine.
I'm sorry I can't make it better –
it's all I want to do.

Mel and I stay out all day,
eating chips and trying on clothes
I can't afford.
She buys a load of stuff
and tries to buy me things,
but I'm not having it.

We walk down the high street,
Mel weighed down with bags
full of the latest gear,
past an old lady sitting in a doorway
surrounded by everything she owns
and a middle-aged man asleep on a bench.

A young woman,
she can't be much older than us,
sits outside Costa
with a cardboard sign
asking for money.

I can't make eye contact with her,
wondering,

if Dad can't find us somewhere to live,
how close are we to becoming homeless?

A group of boys sit on benches
in the middle of town, being loud and
throwing cans of cider.

Isn't that Ryan? Mel asks.

Yeah it is.
I stand looking at him, confused.
A lady with a burkha walks past them
and one of the boys throws a can at her.
She ducks,
the can narrowly missing her head.

Surprised you could see it coming,
one of them says.
The group laughs and
her pace quickens.

Mel tries to pull me away.
But I stand there, staring,
wanting Ryan to see me,
unable to get my head round
what **I've seen**.

I've seen the light
under the door fade and
wonder when it will be time to leave.

A few minutes later,
another man arrives.
He says his name is Farid,
and he's our smuggler.

Hurry up, he says. *We leave now.*

One by one
we leave the dark room.
We're to make this journey on foot.

We'll be in Kassala before you know it,
Tesfay whispers.

I force a smile.

Darkness cloaks the city
as our journey as illegal migrants begins.
Teseney to Kassala.

It will take all night
and we must stay in the
shadows.

At the Sudanese border
there are mines and guards.
Shoot to kill,
no hesitation.

From now on,
our lives are
worthless.

313 days before

Mel hugs me tight
outside our form room.
You look like shit, babe, she says.

I didn't sleep.

Still thinking about that stuff in town yesterday?

Yeah.
I'm exhausted.

You need to forget it.
Just boys being idiots.
Nothing you can do about it.

But this is serious, Mel.
These new friends he's hanging with,
I don't recognize them.

He's got new friends, so what?

They looked and sounded like trouble, Mel.
What they said to that woman, it was disgusting.

Ryan didn't actually say anything though . . .

But if he's hanging with people who are saying stuff like that,
isn't it just as bad?

Mel's quiet for a moment.
Yeah, you're right . . .

Mum would always say, 'You're complicit in your silence.'
And I know Ryan changed after Mum's diagnosis,
and we've been fighting and stuff,

but that wasn't right, Mel, what I saw yesterday.
That's not Ryan.

The bell rings
and Mel and I make our way to sociology.
My head is swimming and I'm
feeling completely out of my depth.

My head is swimming and I'm
feeling completely out of my depth.
We follow Farid in single file,
holding on to each other in the dark.
I can't see the ground beneath my feet
or the hand in front of my face.

The night is full of shadows,
and the sound of hyenas
has my heart racing.
We stumble
fall
cry
twist
climb
under
and
over
as branches and thorns
tear at skin.
I bite my bottom lip
to stop myself from crying.
I look up at the night sky
and **I stare into**   **space**.

I stare into   **space**
as Miss Adams discusses
crime and social hierarchy.
Everyone's chipping in
with thoughts and statistics.

Socio-economic this
and global that –

I like sociology.
I only took it because of Mel –
I chose all the same subjects as her.
It feels like we don't do much work,
we just talk a lot
and then get slapped with an essay
once a term.

I never join in.
I just listen.
Take it in,
make notes.
Mel's all over it.
I love watching her;
she's so articulate
and sparky.
It's well sexy.

I read that hate crimes are on the rise, Miss.
Why is that?

That's an excellent question, Melissa, and ties in nicely
with crime and the disenfranchisement of people.
There's no one reason, but often it's feeling voiceless,
feeling like second-class citizens in their 'own' country
that leads to people joining far-right groups.

She starts writing a list on the board
and Mel squeezes my hand.

Ryan's not a fucking Nazi, I whisper.

I'm not saying he is, she whispers back.

Any more from the class?

And everyone
starts calling out . . .
       unemployment

                poverty

   education

                    health care.

It's like the whole class knows Ryan better than me.
I guess it's easy when you're on the outside looking **in**.

In the darkness
the sky is bathed in starlight.

          Why is that star so bright, Baba?

          That, Sammy, is the North Star.
          And do you know why it's important?

          Because it's the brightest?

          It's a landmark. A marker in the sky.
          If you're lost or you need guidance,
          just look up, find this star
          and it will lead you towards hope.

          Why do you love the stars so much, Baba?

          Because it's where we come from.

          I thought we came from our mamas?

          Yes, we do. He laughs. But if we think a little deeper,
          humans are created from the same materials that are present
          in the stars. We're all just stardust, Sammy.

We continue through thorny bushes
and over stony ground

with only the stars as our guide.
Another six hours **we're told**.

We're told that
people think this country is changing.
They feel like second-class citizens and
they're angry that they're being left behind,
politics causing a bigger gap
between the haves and the have-nots,
and
if you didn't have much to begin with anyway
you're gonna start looking for someone to
blame.

I try to see,
try and understand.
But Ryan and I
share the same blood,
we come from the same place, so
if I don't think like that,
how can he? **I think**.

I think about crossing the border.
I think about the country I'm leaving behind,
the country that murdered Baba and
won't tell us what happened to Sophia.

I think of the UK.
I think of all the things I can
become, do, change and create.
I try and imagine
the life I could live.

We're a mathematical anomaly . . .
Once you realize the statistical odds of our existence . . .
it should remind you of all the possibilities that exist in us.

I try and see
the endless possibilities
as we claw through the darkness,
looking up at the stars.

Looking up at the stars
from my bedroom window,
my eyes are drawn to the brightest one.

> *Close your eyes, Nat . . . keep them closed . . . no peeking . . .*
> *Now open them!*

> *A cake! Thanks, Ry . . .*

> *Not any old cake. Cut into it . . .*

> *A rainbow cake!*

> *Couldn't have you come out*
> *and not celebrate the moment. Listen, if any of those kids at school*
> *give you a hard time, you tell me, all right . . .?*

> *I can handle it . . .*

> *I mean it. I've got your back.*
> *I'm not having anyone*
> *spewing any ignorant bullshit and hate.*
> *I've gotta stick up for my little sis.*

I'm still awake when I hear
Ryan come home at 3 a.m.
Curtains not drawn,
I continue looking at the stars.

I continue looking at the stars.

I'm awake till

        I'm awake till

sunrise.

        sunrise.

312 days before

We're in Sudan.
The landscape is a burst of yellow and orange.
My heart feels as though
it's taking its last beats.

We're exhausted.
Our legs, arms and feet
are a bloody mess.
Battered, bruised,
scratched to the bone.

Not a soul in sight.
Farid points to a hut.
Wait in there, he orders.

We sit close to one another,
our collective hearts racing,
waiting for the next order,
our next move.

We hear the sound of a vehicle.
Farid bursts in with three other men.
It all happens so quickly.

First they tie our hands,
second they blindfold us,
third Kalashnikovs digging into our backs,
fourth our trembling bodies
are shoved into a truck.
A truck that is already packed
with **desperate people**.

Desperate people sit waiting
for the meeting to start.

There are about a hundred of us
crammed into Orchid House.
The TV screen springs to life.

We watch shiny people
with silky voices
sell us a dream.

The houses look beautiful,
so big and bright,
with front and back gardens.
I imagine a new bedroom,
sitting in an open-plan kitchen.
I smile, thinking I'd live closer to Mel.

Prospect Homes are the future.
Prospect Homes promise paradise.
The video comes to an end.

I nudge Dad.
They look amazing, I whisper.
He squeezes my hand,
flicking through the brochure,
the smile fading from his face
as he turns each page.

Councillor Emery stands in front of us,
perfect blonde bob,
smart grey suit,
like someone out of a
payday-loan advert.

It's fantastic to see such a wonderful turnout, she says.
But her smile,
suit
and perfect blonde bob
can't hold the desperate people back.

How many homes are available to people who live in the area?

How many? Say a number!

Ten years ago they built affordable housing and they said fifty per cent was for social. In the end it was only five per cent!

Can you tell us what affordability is? In the brochure it says that the prices start at £250,000. How can anyone here afford that?!

What about renting?!

Councillor Emery's
perfect blonde bob
wilts under the heat
of one hundred angry people.

Why can't you give a straight answer?

Ryan's out of his seat.
So basically none of us here can afford what you're showing us!

Sit down, Ryan.

No, Dad. Why have you come here today if you can't offer us anything!

The room erupts in chaos and
two burly men take Ryan,
kicking and shouting,
out of **the door**.

The door is locked with chains.
We're in a prison of sorts,
driven for hours,
disorientated and exhausted.
There are twenty of us in total,
all wearing the same look of horror,
all Eritrean.

Where are we?

We only drove for a few hours. We're most likely still in Sudan,
whispers Yonas.

They're going to kill us, I know it.
There's no way Mama can get the money for a ransom.

So much for my new life,
my dreams
of **paradise**.

Paradise *they call it.*
I believed it an' all.
Turned out to be a load of crap.
Ryan kicked off and got chucked out.

I'm sorry, babe.
She squeezes me into her and
I allow myself to soften.

Come on, she says,
taking my hand,
walking towards the water's edge.
I become more and more frightened
the closer we get;
it's been months since I stepped into the sea.

Just take your shoes off, roll up your jeans
and step in. That's all you have to do.

Can't you leave me to do it in my own time?

If I left you to do that, we'd be waiting all year.
You know you want to – it's in your blood.

I'm frozen
to

the
spot.

Just your feet, nothing else.
You're just dipping your toes in, that's all,
nothing more.
I'm here, holding your hand.
I'm not going to let go.

She gives careful instructions.

Shoes off . . .
Now socks . . .
Roll up your jeans . . .
Ready?

Ready.

We start walking towards the water,
the pebbles under my feet
hurting.
The water
laps at my toes,
Mel's hand
tight round mine.
I step back.

It's OK, she says. *It's OK.*

I take a breath,
step forward,
keep stepping
till the cold water
laps at my ankles.

See, you're doing it. I'm so proud of you.

I keep walking
till the water touches my calves.

I let go of her hand.
I keep walking
till the water laps at my knees.
I keep walking.

Hey! she shouts.
What are you doing?

I keep walking
till I'm up to my thighs,
my waist.
I feel the blood pumping
through my veins again.
I can feel my heart beating again.
I can feel it filling up.
I keep walking
up to my chest.

I hear Mel shouting,
Don't go any deeper!
I keep walking.
The stones suddenly drop away
and I'm fully submerged.

I don't fight it.
I stay under,
feel the water surrounding me,
feel the particles that washed round Mum
wash round me.
I breathe out slowly and sink deeper.

I open my eyes and see her.
My water baby, she says.
I hold out my hand, wanting to touch her.
Mum . . .

Suddenly, an arm round my neck
drags me out of the sea.
What the fuck was that?!

Mel holds my shoulders and shakes me.
Look at me. What the fuck was that?!

Sorry . . . I'm sorry . . .
*I was just trying to feel **something**.*

312 days before

We're tied in chains,
held at gunpoint
and beaten,
forced to call our families
during the torture.

If we don't pay, we'll be sold
or murdered –
it makes no difference to them.
A fifteen-thousand-dollar ransom.
The cost of a life.

But mine and Tesfay's families
have just about managed
to find the money
we needed to get us to Europe.

It would be impossible
to ask for **more**.

    More of them coming here every day. It's a joke.

        My sister can't get a flat cos of them. She's in a hostel.
        Two kids an' all.

    How's the job hunting, Ryan?

It's a joke. I'm on this zero-hours crap. I don't get anything.

        Too right it's a joke. I'm down the job centre every day, mate.
        Every fucking day, right, but they don't wanna know. I don't tick
        the right fucking boxes.

Too fucking right. You have to come to the pub next
Wednesday, Ryan. You have to meet Danny. He's a
proper geezer. Sees it like it is. We're second-class
citizens in our own country and he ain't afraid to say it.

Dunno, mate, all sounds a bit heavy to me.

Listen. There's no one sticking up for us. Since when have we
had anything? I've been sleeping on a couch for three years.
You been kicked out your house, Ryan. We need to stick up for
ourselves, we're the ones losing out.

Shit's gonna go down. I'm telling ya, Danny's gonna
change things around here. Just come, Ryan.

I know what you're thinking, but it ain't racist to want what
should be ours.

All right . . . yeah . . . I'll come.

That's my boy! Next Wednesday, seven p.m.,
the Red Lion.

I listen at the door.
My breath held.

My breath held
as each lash comes down on my back.
I try and hold in the pain.
The whip comes down
again and again.
I try and hold it in,
but when my skin splits
I scream.

Stop, please stop! I'll get you everything you ask for,
I hear Mama scream.
Everything!

304 days before

Seven days have passed.
Tesfay and I have not been sold
yet.
We're still alive,
but we won't be
if our families
can't find the money
to free us.

We're called slaves,
barely given any food or water,
beaten daily and
locked in a shed with chains
round our ankles.

Yanos, Petros and Hamid –
one by one –
taken.
Where to?
Dead
or free?

A family
torn apart
once again.

We are
trapped,
helpless and hopeless.

Helpless and hopeless.
That's how I feel,
standing at the door,
seeing them all in the lounge –

Ryan and his new mates.
Laughing at something on the laptop.

It's been the same every day this week.
I come home from school to
a gang of lads in the front room.
I told Dad, but he said they're just harmless
and we've gotta be gentle with Ryan
because he's working stuff out.

But this is not being gentle.
This is brushing a massive pile of shit
under the carpet,
and just because you can't see it
doesn't mean
it isn't gonna stink.

I can hear you creeping around!
Come in here and watch this! Ryan shouts.

No thanks! I shout back,
then add *'prick'* under my breath.

I close my bedroom door
and climb into bed.
I can pretend I'm in a whole new world in here,
with my photos, fairy lights
and fake stars on the ceiling.
I look at a photo of all four of us
on the wall by my pillow.

Haaapy birrrrthdaaay, dear Na-aaat!
Haaappy birrthdaaay toooo youuuuuu!

You don't have to sing to your sister every time she
walks into a room, Ryan.

I think I do! Them's the rules when it's my favourite sister's birthday.

I'm your only sister.

Same thing! Right, I've planned the whole day, sis,
but it's a surprise so you've got to go with it, OK?

OK!

This is a big day. You're becoming a teenager, Nat.
Look at this face, Mum, Dad.
Take it in. Appreciate it, cos we've got exactly twenty-hours
before she turns all pimply and moody . . .

Well, you've not been too bad, Ryan,
so you never know – we might be lucky with Nat.

We need to leave now, Mum, otherwise we'll be late for the first
surprise.

All right, Ryan. Anyone would think it was your birthday.
Oh, but before we leave let's take a photo.
Say cheese . . .

I hear an eruption of laughter
from downstairs,
put on some music
and drown out **the noise**.

The noise of the chains on the door
wakes us from a restless sleep.
Get up! the man demands.
I stand, shivering.
Hurry up! he spits,
poking me with a stick.
I look back at Tesfay.
This could be the last time I see him.
Move, he demands
and pushes me
into the dead of **night**.

Nights are coming in quicker.
I always feel a sense of loss
as the days get shorter.

Mel meets me in town
and we head over to the pub.
Ryan left the house an hour ago, I say.

We stand on the opposite side of the road.
I'm too scared to cross.
Come on, now or never.
Mel takes my hand.

Please don't be there,
I say to myself.
Please don't be there.

But there he is,
clear as day,
sitting at a table by the window
with his new mates.

There's a man
shouting through a microphone,
men and women
nodding along.
The longer I look at Ryan,
the uglier he gets.

The man with the mic draws everyone in.
Mark, how long your sister been looking for a flat?
Two years! It's a disgrace.
Lucy darling, how many GCSEs you got?
Seven GCSEs, people. A bright young woman like Lucy
can't get a job.
And Ryan, mate, how long you been job hunting?
A year and you're been kicked out of your house an' all,
yeah? Good luck finding a new place.
Everyone, I'd like you to meet Ryan, our newest recruit.

Everyone looks over at Ryan
and raises their pint glasses.

I'm Danny. I'll be at the bar.
Thank you and goodnight!
He does a mic drop
like he's a fucking rock star.
The pub erupts in laughter and cheers.

Ryan gets up,
goes to the bar
and shakes Danny's hand.
Danny ruffles Ryan's hair,
slaps him on the back
and buys him a **pint**.

283 days before

I have lost count
of the days,
weeks.

Last night I was tied up
and held upside down
for hours.

Whipped,
electrocuted,
cut.

Mama
heard
every
scream.

> *Whatever happens, Sammy,*
> *do not forget*
> *how to love,*
> *your worth,*
> *who you are,*
> *how to feel.*
> *Keep checking,*
> *because when you see awful sights –*
> *and you will –*
> *these are the things that are easy to forget.*

Every inch of my skin
screams in pain,
but I'm still here.
I'm still alive.
I know how to love.
I know my worth.
I know who I am.

I know and feel all these things.
The most important thing
is to continue to **feel**.

Feels heavy
in the house tonight.
Dad's on the computer,
trying to fill in the benefits forms
since his hours have been cut at work.

They don't make it easy for you.
I've been at this for over two hours.
It's like they don't want you to get help.

Dad, I need to tell you something about Ryan.

You've got to stop worrying about him, Nat.
He's eighteen. He can look after himself.

I can't help feeling
like I've lost
two parents.
Dad's here
but absent.
He looks old,
worry trickling down
the lines in his face,
burying itself in the creases.

What's going on now?
It's frozen – the screen's frozen!

He grabs the computer and shakes it,
picks up a stack of letters,
looks at them like they could
smash every dream he's ever had,
stuffs them in a drawer
and heads out.

Ryan comes home a few minutes later,
looking all sorts of hot and bothered.

Are you OK, Ry?
Where've you been?

None of your business. Dad home?

He's just gone out. Why?

Nothing. Erm . . .

His eyes are darting all over the place
and he's sweaty and shaking.

What's happened, Ry?

Nothing. I just went running.

In jeans?

Yes!

He wipes his forehead.

What happened to your hand?

It's nothing. I fell.

We stare at each other.

What have you done, Ryan?

He pushes past me
and legs it upstairs,
leaving a trail of blood
all the way up the **banister**.

282 days before

Straight after registration
we're called into a special assembly.
The whole school.
This only happened once before in Year Seven
when David Price, a kid in Year Ten,
died after falling into a frozen pond
over the Christmas holidays.

We wonder
what news is gonna break.
Mrs Edwards, the head teacher,
stands in front of us.
She clears her throat,
takes a moment
before she speaks.

It is under very sad circumstances I bring you all here today.
Yesterday evening a student from our school was attacked.

There's an intake of breath
from the entire school.

Fazel Mahmood from Year Eleven was viciously attacked and
beaten by a gang of youths in the town centre. He's currently in
hospital. The police are urging anyone who might know anything
to come forward.

I feel
as though
my heart
has stopped.

Fazel.
Fazel from my class.
Fazel. Fazel. Fazel.

I keep saying his name
over   and over   in my head.

I think of Ryan.
His hand.
The blood.
His guilt.

I feel sick to the pit of my stomach.

We walk out of assembly
and I tell Mel about Ryan,
about last night.

He wouldn't.
Ryan's stupid, but he's not a thug.
He's not one of them.

How do we know?

We know. It's Ryan.
You know, goofy Ryan.
Ryan who carves figures out of driftwood.
Ryan who bought you a rainbow cake
to celebrate you coming out.
That Ryan.
The people who did this to Fazel, they're something else.
Trust me.

I wanna see Fazel.
Do you think we'll be allowed?

We can try.

We can try to make a run for it, Sammy.
I can't take this any longer.

How, Tesfay? We're in chains.

He shrugs,
leans back against the wall, wincing,
hunched over like an old man.

Tesfay –
half the size with double the courage –
is shrinking before my **eyes**.

281 days before

Ryan and I sit
at opposite ends of the lounge.

Fucking crazy, isn't it, Nat?

Yeah, it's awful.

No one's forcing them to leave.

That's exactly what they're doing, Ryan.

Whatever, he says.
Believe what you like.
Since when have you started caring more about them than us?

I care about everyone, Ryan.
Didn't you ever listen to Mum?

Mum cared more about them than us as well.

I throw a newspaper at him.
He ducks.
Just as I consider
throwing something else,
the photo of a teenage boy
flashes up on the TV.

Police are still urging witnesses to come forward
in regard to the attack on Fazel Mahmood
two nights ago.

Ryan is silent.
He knocks his knuckles
against the edge of the table.

His cheeks are red,
his eyes narrow.
Both of us with one eye on the news report
and one eye
on
each
other.

I look at the photo
of Fazel on the TV.
I look back at Ryan.

The overheard conversations,
the meeting down the pub,
the blood on his hand.

My heart says no,
Ryan would never . . .
My head says
maybe
Ryan
has
become
'something else'.

My head is spinning.

My head is spinning
from lack of food and water.
It's long after sunset
when Tesfay and I
are unchained and
loaded on to a truck
with a few other people.

We sit crammed together,
our eyes wild with fear.
This is it, I think.
We're being sent to our deaths.

Where are they taking us?
I ask an Eritrean woman crouched next to me.
Khartoum, she says.

The ransom has been paid.
All fifteen thousand dollars.
How did Mama find the money?
I think of all the things my family
must have had to sell,
loans they must have taken out.

I look at Tesfay.
We're free.

280 days before

We visit Fazel.

Mel bought him flowers
and we tentatively
approach his house.
A woman with a grey bob
and a floral dress answers the door.

Hi, I'm Mel and this is Nat. We're friends from school.
We just wanted to see how Fazel was.

Of course, she says,
ushering us in from the outside.
I'm Lorraine, Fazel's foster mum.
Mel and Nat?
He's never mentioned you . . .
Mind you,
he never talks much about school.
She smiles kindly
but her eyes tell a story
of all sorts of sad.
Fazel's in his room resting.
He'll be really happy to have visitors,
I'm sure.

We follow her up the stairs
to Fazel's room.
She knocks gently at the door
before carefully opening it.

Your friends Mel and Nat
are here to see you.
Are you feeling up to it?

Fazel looks over at us,

confused,
but nods.

I try not to look shocked.
I try and keep it together.
His face is badly bruised
and his head is bandaged up.

Mel and I sit,
not really knowing
what to say.

Everyone at school misses you, I say.

Really?

*Really. The whole school is talking about you.
It's all over the news.*

Talking about me doesn't mean caring.

Well . . . we brought you flowers, Mel says
after an awkward silence,
and puts them on the corner of his bed.

Do you remember much of what happened? I ask.

Bits, not lots. Slowly, things come back.

Did you see who did it?

No. It happened so fast.
He closes his eyes.

Sorry, I'll stop asking so many questions, I say.
*I'm really sorry about what happened, Fazel,
and not just this, everything, like at school . . .
The police questioned Kevin Smith.*

You should have seen him.
He looked like he was gonna piss his pants.
Mel laughs nervously.

He doesn't smile.

He doesn't smile.
Our smuggler.
He stands in front of us,
holding a pistol.
Get out! he shouts.

It's still dark
when we arrive in Khartoum.
We scatter like stars,
finding our way through the streets,
past coffee shops,
restaurants and internet cafes.
It seems the city
is ablaze with a million lights.

I didn't know there were so many tall glass buildings, says Tesfay.
Can we stay here?

It's no safer here than Eritrea, not for us anyway.

I know, he says. *Just let me take this in.*
I never thought I'd live to see it.

I look up at the night sky,
the stars like dim light bulbs
in my eyes.

> *No matter how dark it gets, Sammy,*
> *there are still stars in the* **sky**.

279 days before

We're easily spotted
by smugglers.
Men who watch closely
for new arrivals
desperate to cross the desert,
getting us one step closer to
paradise.

One body at a time
like human cargo
we pile into trucks.

Body against body,
breathing together
groaning together
crying together
praying together.

Dear God,
I don't want to die.
I don't want to die.
I don't want to die.

'I DON'T WANT TO DIE.' PLEA OF REFUGEES
RESCUED AFTER BEING STRANDED IN SAHARA DESERT

I fold over the newspaper
and push it away across the kitchen table,
needing a physical   distance
from it, but
I can't ignore it.
I pick it back up,
read the story.
The full horror of it.

The number of refugees dying,
the numbers that don't get accounted for.
I think of Mum.
Slowly,
her job has started to feel
less distant.

> They're just people, Nat,
> like you and me,
> wanting to be safe,
> wanting to be free.

There's an ad at the bottom of the article.

CARE4CALAIS. RAISE MONEY AND HELP REFUGEES.

Care4Calais?
I google it before I even know why.

**We help millions of refugees fleeing
war and persecution.
All over the world, providing aid
and long-term accommodation.
Donate here . . .
Ideas to raise money here . . .**

I click through and as I'm reading
I start feeling something
waking up
inside me.
*Bike rides, marathons, swims, mountain climbs,
fashion shows, cake sales . . .* the list is endless.
My eyes land on *swims*.
Channel relay – done that.
Lake Windermere – done that too.
Solo Channel swim.
I stare at the words for a long time.
Could I?
No. I shake my head. No way.

I think about the water,
getting in without Mum,
training alone.
I can't –
it would be too hard.

I sit reading the story
a couple more times.
I hear Mum's voice willing me on.
You can do anything you put your mind to, Natty.

I think of all the reasons I couldn't do it:
I'm not good enough.
It's too far!
A Channel relay is one thing,
but this . . . this is all Mum.
No way could *I* do it.
I'm not on a swimming scholarship any more.
Who would train me?
Where would I even get the money?

I think about Fazel,
wanting to help,
wanting to do something good.
I think about Mum and
how this was going to be her challenge.
I think about Ryan,
his hate,
how far we've drifted from each other.

I shake my head.
I can't let Ryan stop me.
It's because of him and his mates
that I have to do it.
The words hit me.
I *have* to do it.

I sit back in the kitchen chair.
Could I really do it?
Could I really finish what she started? **I think.**

I think of nothing
but the next moment.
We breathe
the oppressive heat,
panting in and out,
pleading for water,
melting into one another.

Tesfay and I
talk of God
and sometimes
I think **I see him**.

I see him.
Sitting with a gang
in town.
I want to shake him.
When did you get so lost, Ryan?
I stare at him for a long time.
I want him to look like he doesn't belong.
I want him to look sad,
lost, desperate.
It's the only way I can make sense of it all
and believe
this isn't him.

This isn't him.
Tesfay, who's usually
so talkative, has been so quiet.
I nudge him awake.
He's sound asleep.
It's the best way to be, I think.
He's conserving his energy.
In the night, when the truck
feels like a refrigerator,
I hold Tesfay tight,
keep his ice-cold body **warm**.

Warm Indian summers result in warm water.
As warm as the Dover seas can get.
It's mid-October and
I haven't told anyone about my Channel swim idea.
It felt weird keeping it from Mel all day.
For now, the secret is mine.
I need to get into the water.
I need to swim again.

My first swim
without Mum.
My first attempt
as a Channel swimmer.

Maybe.

Tonight is about me.
Tonight is about getting in the water.
Tonight is about seeing what's possible.

I wear Mum's swimsuit and cap –
It feels like she's with me.

I step into the sea.
It's cold.
It's refreshing, Nat – that's what Mum would say.
Everything inside is telling me to
go back –
this isn't my place any more.
It doesn't feel right doing it alone,
but a whisper urges me on.
One more step, Nat, go on.

I step deeper and deeper
from ankles
to knees
to thighs
to waist
to chest

to neck
to head.
I am under.

Murky blue-brown
swirling round my head,
eyes open,
I look into nothing.
Feeling the cold penetrate my skin
gives rise to something
that's been buried
for too long.

I scream.
I scream into the water.
I scream out the grief
the anger
the hurt
the sorrow
the confusion
the despair
the helplessness.

I scream and scream and scream,
and sink and sink and sink,
coming up
new.

278 days before

If anyone can do it, you can, Nat.

Yeah, but this is crossing the whole Channel, Mel.

You've done half the distance before
at Lake Windermere.

It's not the same with currents and stuff.

Didn't an eleven-year-old do it once?

Yeah.

So you're sixteen with swimming experience. Scholarship,
the Channel relay, all them lakes – you're a fish, babe.

That's what Mum used to say.

We're silent.

I really miss your mum.
If it wasn't for her, we probably wouldn't be together.

I know. I think about that too.

Mum had bought tickets for *Dreamgirls*
at the Marlowe in Canterbury,
a birthday treat.

But she felt too sick to go –
we didn't know then just how serious it was.
So I asked Mel instead.
I fancied her,
but I didn't think she'd be interested.
We were
just mates.

As soon as the lights came down,
it was clear there was something between us.
There was a charge in the air
and during Effie's song in Act Two
something electric happened.
Mel took my hand in hers.

Is that OK?
Her breath hot in my ear
sends a shiver down my spine.

Yeah, it's OK.

Phew, thought I'd read the signals wrong.

Heart beating,
cheeks flushing
as my hand closes round hers.

Mel's got her notebook out,
scribbling down a list.

Right . . . she says, looking like a sexy secretary.
I can totally help you raise the sponsorship money.
I can set up a page for you, link it to my Insta and,
if every one of my followers just gave a pound,
you'd have enough for the registration and
boat hire and raise over two grand for Care4Calais.

It all seems a bit too easy.

It's not easy, but it's doable.
Anything is, once you put your mind to it.
You know that better than anyone.

Dunno how I'm gonna pay for the training.

I'm sure school will still help out.

I'm not on the team this year.

All you have to do is ask.

I swallow my frustration.
Mel's don't-ask-don't-get attitude annoys me.
Everything always seems so easy for her.
If she was doing this swim, she wouldn't need
to raise money for boat hire,
or think about a Saturday job to pay for training.

I look round her bedroom
and think there's probably
2,000 pounds' worth
of clothes in her wardrobe.
I hate myself for resenting
everything she has.

*Once you've got a date for the swim,
we can go live, she says.*

I feel overwhelmed by the task.

What's wrong, Nat?

*I wish I hadn't said anything. It's a stupid idea –
there's no way I can swim the Channel.
I don't know what I was thinking.*

She takes me over
to her bedroom mirror.

*Look at yourself.
Try seeing what I see.
You're so strong, Nat.
You've been through so much
and you keep going.
There's nothing you can't do.*

Maybe it's time to start growing
into the person you really are.

I stare at myself in her mirror.
There I am, I think. *There **I am**.*

I am breathing through a gap in the window.
The sun rises and we roast.
A baby cries out in hunger.

I am breathing through a gap in the window.
The truck starts and stops
yet the doors never open.

I am breathing through a gap in the window.
The ground is hard and rocky.
We go up and down, our bodies battered.

I am breathing through a gap in the window.
A young boy falls from the truck.
Stop! we scream. *Stop!*
But the truck keeps **going**.

Going to visit Fazel
after school and telling him about my idea
puts a smile on my face, and
I hope it'll put one on his too.

I'm talking excitedly
about how much I'll need to train.
Fazel sits up in bed.
I think he's impressed.

. . . and Mel says she can take charge of all the fundraising.

He's quiet.

So . . . what do you think?

Do you care what I think?

I shrug my shoulders.
I can't help feeling a little
annoyed.

You want me to say thank you?
To bow down and show gratitude?

No . . . I just . . .

Suddenly visiting me.
Now a charity swim.
You're saving me,
is that it?

No, of course not.

Where were you when Kevin Smith threw his pens?
Or took away my chair?
And when everyone laughed at the drawing on the board,
where were you?
You watched me fall.
Every time, you and your friend Mel,
you watched me fall.

I'm sorry . . .

I don't need your sorry.
I'm not some weak little refugee.
It's only when I'm beaten to the ground
that you decide to look down and see me.
We're not weak.
You don't flee from war and persecution
and survive
if you're weak.
You know what's just as bad as bullies?

People like you. What do they call you?
White saviours. That's it.
At least with a bully you know where you stand.
You, you have your own agenda.
Appease your guilt some other way.
Do your swim,
raise your money,
get your certificate,
*but leave me the hell **alone**.*

Alone. In. Thoughts.
Pictures. Of. Death.
No. Food. In. Forty. Hours.
Thirst. Is. Worse.
Body. Is. Swollen.
Skin. On. Fire.
Sand. In. Gums.
Tongue. Dry.
I. Am. Not. Thirsty.
I. Am. Not. Thirsty.
I. Am. Not. Thirsty.
Over. And. Over.

Over and over
Fazel's words play on a loop
in my head.
I don't have another agenda.
I'm not trying to be a white saviour, I tell myself.
My defences are up.
He's got me wrong.
I'm not who he thinks I am.
Or **am I?**

Am. I. Human?
Do. I. Feel?
Am. I. Worthy?

Do. I. Love?

I look at Tesfay.
Hey, brother, keep the faith, he says,
sounding like there's gravel in his throat.

Yes, I whisper to myself.
Despite it all, *Yes.*
There. Are. Still. Stars. In. The. **Dark**.

277 days before

I think that's brilliant, Nat!
Dad gives me a massive hug.

It wouldn't cost us anything.
Mel said boat hire can come out of the
sponsorship money that's raised.

Your mum would be so proud.

I was wondering about getting her coach to train me.
I'll get a job weekends, after school, anything I can find.
I'll pay for it all.
Plus I've got old training plans from the relay and Windermere,
so I can work off those.
I can probably do a lot of it on my own
and with Mel's help.

What about me?

What about you?

Well . . . I could train you.

You?!

It's not that ridiculous an idea.

But you've never done it before.

Training was all your mum ever talked about.
Plus there's the internet and your old swim coach,
Mr . . . Mr . . .

Mr Watkins.

Yeah, I'm sure he'd help draw up a plan.

I don't know, Dad.

I've got your mum's diary.
She'd planned her training down to a T.

Erm . . .

I could do with having something to focus on, Nat.
I think this would be good for me and . . . us.
Make up for some lost time.
What do you say?

OK. OK. Let's do it.

Thanks, love. I think we'll make a great team.

How could I say no?
When your dad's standing in front of you,
asking to be saved,
how can you say no?

We need to find a pilot, book a spot.
It probably won't be for a couple of years.

No problem, Nat. I can look into that.

When should we start?

*How about **today**?*

Today is the third day
                              maybe.
Doors open.
Ahhh.
My. Eyes. Can't. Take. The. Light.

Bodies fall out,
tumbling on to the
desert sand
like bread rolls.

Sammy? Sammy?
Tesfay sounds so distant.
I feel him shake me.
Sammy, Sammy!

Water, he needs water,
I hear him say.
He drags me out of the truck.
You need to stay awake, Sammy.
Here, drink this water.

No sooner does the cup reach my lips
than it is snatched out of his hands.

What do you think you're doing?
Why waste it – are you stupid?

He needs water, pleads Tesfay.

He's nearly dead, you idiot.
Leave him and drink the water yourself.

Nearly dead is not dead! Tesfay shouts.

And then I feel it.
Water
on my lips,
down my throat.

Thank you, brother, I say weakly
and close my eyes **again**.

Again! Dad shouts.

Again? I'm tired, Dad.

That was just the warm-up. Come on.
If you're gonna get fit for the Channel,
you've gotta keep practising. How much do you want this?

You know how much.

Well then, stop being a mardy arse and get swimming.
Half an hour more, then you're done.

I battle through every drill,
every stroke,
my shoulders burning.

My shoulders burning.
My legs swollen.
My skin on fire.
Our smuggler pokes us with his rifle.

Get in or stay here and end up like your friends, he says.

Can we at least bury them? a woman asks.

No, we're leaving. You want to bury them,
you can make your own way across the desert.

Tesfay helps me into the truck.
There are four fewer people and
I can stretch out my legs a little,
too dehydrated for tears,
thinking how awful it is that
I'm grateful
I can stretch out **my legs**.

My legs feel heavy and tired
as Dad and I walk into the house
and kick off our shoes.

That was fun, wasn't it, Nat?

Yeah, Dad, you're a great coach.

He smiles like a kid
who's just come first on sports day.

Right, I'll get dinner on.
And he strides into the kitchen
with a real spring in his step.
Ryan's sitting in the lounge.

Where you two been?

Swimming.

Thought you said you were giving that up.

Changed my mind.

I crash on the sofa
and flick through TV channels.
The local news is all about
the boats –
another two arrived this morning.
Ryan tuts.
I ignore him.

Dad comes in half an hour later.
Right, I've just called Terry.
He was gonna be your mum's pilot.
He's got two slots.
He pauses.

What, Dad?

*Third week in July next year
or second week in August the year after.*

July next year. That's crazy, Dad. That only gives me nine months.

It's up to you, love. You've got more experience than most.

What would Mum do?

I think you know.

I need to think about it, Dad.

OK, love. Terry said he has to know by tomorrow.

Ryan's head bats
to and fro
from me to Dad.

Anyone gonna tell me what's going on?

*Your sister's swimming the Channel.
Raising money for a charity that helps refugees.
We had our first training session today.
Went well, didn't it, Nat? She said I make a great coach an' all!
Your mum would be so proud, love.
It's good, isn't it, having something to focus on?
Yeah . . . it feels good.
You could learn something from Nat, Ryan.
Get yourself off the sofa and set yourself a goal or something.*

And then he's back in the kitchen.
I think I can hear him singing.

Are you for fucking real?

What, Ry?

You know what. We're being kicked out of our house
and this is what you care about?

They're two separate things, Ry.

He's calm like he's trying to teach me something.

Are they?
Have you ever thought they're the reason we can't get
a council house?
Why I can't get a job?

No, Ryan. No, I haven't. Cos it's a load of crap.
Is that what your new mate Danny is telling you?

Yeah, and he knows about politics and stuff.
You'll see soon enough.

I will, will I?

Yeah.

He looks at me
like it's a threat.
I call Dad.

What, love?

Tell Terry I'll go for July.

You sure?

Yep.

OK, love. Right, I'd better start making a plan. Exciting!
What do you say, Ryan?
Should we celebrate our Nat here with her favourite takeaway?

Ryan shakes his head,
bites his bottom lip
and looks at me like
he doesn't want to know **me**.

276 days before

Mel and I are supposed to be having a date night,
but instead she's setting up my social-media presence.

Darling, would you like a snack?

Mel's mum hovers at the bedroom door.

No thanks, Mum.

Hello, Natalie darling.
How are you?

I'm OK, thanks, Mrs Gee.

Well, just shout if you need anything.

We're fine, Mum. Bye.
Mel eyeballs her mum out of the room.
God, sorry. She just doesn't know when to leave.

I didn't mind, I say,
wishing my mum was at home
making me snacks.

Shall we finish this in the summer house?
I think I need to see the sea for inspiration.

Yeah, sure, I say,
resisting the urge to roll my eyes.
Lately, I'm finding myself
getting more and more
pissed off,
feeling envious of all the things she has,
mostly jealous she still has a mum.

Mel opens the doors to the summer house
and it's like stepping into another world.
It's covered floor to ceiling in fairy lights.

Wow. It's beautiful, Mel.

*I thought, well, if we can't go out,
I'll bring date night to us.*

I feel like a complete bitch.

I was thinking, she says,
pouring me a can of Coke
and putting some snacks on a plate,
*people need to hear your story.
That's how they'll connect to you and want to donate.*

What have I got to say?

*Loads. You could, if you wanted, talk about your mum.
Her job. How she inspired you. How you're finishing what she started.*

I'm not sure.

It's up to you. It was just a suggestion.

I've never really spoken about her.

I know it's difficult. I can help you write something if you like?

Where do I even start?

*From the **beginning**.*

Beginning another day with
a dry mouth
a dry tongue
a throbbing head

a moaning stomach
a groaning throat.

Water runs low,
our bodies
drying out in the **heat**.

275 days before

Someone is rocking back and forth.
Someone is crying.
Someone is vomiting.
Someone feels cold in the midday sun.
Someone is screaming.
Someone speaks to God.
Someone sings.
Someone hasn't moved.

I've lost count of the days
as I drift in and out
of **this nightmare**.

THIS NIGHTMARE! HOW MANY MORE
BOATLOADS CAN WE TAKE?

I see the headline on the board
outside a newsagent's on my way to school.

Refugee lover,
Kevin shouts across the classroom.
Mel told me to expect some hate.
My page went live yesterday and I've already
raised one hundred pounds,
donated by Mel's mum and dad –
of course.

*My dad says there's people that need help here
and you're helping a bunch of freeloaders.*

I bite my tongue,
my face burning.

My dad says most of these countries don't even have a war going on –
the people just want our benefits and jobs.

Mel turns round and faces him.

Leave it, Mel. Ignore him, I whisper.

Silence is being complicit, isn't that what you said?
she whispers back and then turns to face Kevin.

Which one is it, shit-for-brains?
Benefits or jobs?

Well . . . er . . . half and half . . .

They wouldn't make a terrifying journey for benefits and jobs.
They're risking their lives.
Have you any idea what the journey is like?
It's not the high-speed train up to St Pancras, you prick!

Everyone starts shouting,
Fight! Fight! Fight!

Come on then,
you stupid lezza.

Kevin's out of his seat,
trying to provoke.
I attempt to hold Mel back,
but she's up
and walking over to him.

It's lesbian, you ignorant shithead.

Whack!
Kevin's on the floor
with Mel standing over him,
ready to throw another punch.

And don't you ever start on my girlfriend again.

Whack.

I'm. In. **Love**.

Tesfay, *Tesfay.*

Huh?

Are we alive? Or is this hell?

It's hell on earth, Sammy.

Tesfay?

Huh?

I can't feel.

My body is also numb.

No. I can't feel. I'm somewhere between this place and the next.

Don't say that, Sammy.

It wouldn't be so bad if I fell off this tr–

*Don't say it, Sammy. Don't say **it**.*

It's *the best thing ever, Dad.*
Mr Watkins said they'd do a sponsored swim-a-thon
and Mrs Khooner is gonna get her students in home economics
to bake like a hundred cakes for a bake sale.

A hundred?!

Well . . . I dunno . . . loads anyway, and Mrs Edwards mentioned it
in assembly and everyone clapped, it was so embarrassing . . .
And Mel's socials are . . .

Ryan comes into the kitchen.
I stop.
Zip up my mouth.

All right, Ryan? Did you work today? asks Dad.

Nope.

Are you ringing all the agencies?

Yes.

Did you go to the job centre?

Yes! he snaps.

All right, Ryan, less of the attitude.
I just wanna make sure you're doing everything you can.
Take a leaf out of Nat's book – find yourself some get-up-and-go.

I feel Ryan's stare
burn right through me.

I'm on your side, Ryan.
Sorry, Nat, what was that you were saying about socials?

I talk quickly.
Mel's socials are on fire. We're getting loads of likes.
She doesn't think I'll have a problem getting the sponsorship.
I swear the teachers are being nicer to me.
That Mr Pinnock, who HATES me, actually smiled at me the other day.

It's safe, is it, all this online stuff?

Yeah, Dad, chill.

Ryan leaves the table.
Fuck this, he mutters under his breath.
I'm going out.

When will you be back?

Don't act like you care, Dad.
And
he's
gone.

What did I say?!

I shrug.
With Ryan gone,
I feel like I can breathe again.

Dad and I talk for ages.
We actually have a laugh,
and for the first time
neither of us
feels **guilty**.

273 days before

Bit by bit
we're starved.
Bit by bit
we feel less human.
Bit by bit
we're broken down.
Bit by bit ...

Bit by bit
I build strength and stamina.
Bit by bit
Dad and I rebuild our relationship.
Bit by bit
we lose Ryan.
Bit by bit

bit by bit

bit by **bit**.

272 days before

Day seven in the desert.
No sooner do I open my eyes,
I want to close them again.

Stay with me, Sammy. You have to keep fighting.
Tesfay slaps my cheeks.

Is this what it feels like to die, Tesfay?

It wouldn't be so bad, **I think**.

***I think** I should film all your training sessions
so people can see the amount of hard work you're putting in.*

Mel watches all my training
from the viewing gallery,
cheering me on.
Dad shouts from the side of the pool.
Four nights a week training and at weekends.
This is my life for the next nine months.

I'm the happiest I've been in ages
even though
**my body
aches**.

**My body
aches**.
Sand-filled gums
feel like needles in my teeth.

Look, look!
someone says.
Look, look!

I try to lift my head
and look out of the window.
I can't.

What is it, Tesfay?
My voice
nothing more
than a whisper.

He looks back at me, smiling.

Mountains, brother!
We are close.

Excitement grows,
the sun sinks,
the air turns cold,
as we drive towards
the gateway to **paradise**.

271 days before

Tripoli is full of malls,
white facades,
high-rises and palaces.

We check into a cheap hotel
at separate times –
all sixty of us.
No one asks for papers.

For the first time in a week,
I see my reflection in the mirror.
I look like a ghost.
Sunken and hollow.
Thin skin on bone.
A face and body
so close to death.

I scrub myself clean,
try to wash away the horror,
but the nightmare plays in my head
on **a loop**.

A loop –
*swim from the beach towards the eastern block halfway along the
harbour wall,
then across to the western block and back to the beach.
That should take an hour and a half,
then you can take a break and repeat the loop.
Got it?* Dad asks.

Got it,
I repeat.

I repeat
the conversation in my mind,
determined to hold on to
the sound of her voice.

Mama. I made it to Tripoli.

Oh, Sammy!

I'm safe. I'm well.

You promise?

I promise.

And Tesfay?
Are you looking after him?

He's the one looking after me, Mama.
You know he has twice the strength.

Look after each other.

There's so much more to say,
but the money runs out.
I quickly add,
I love you,
before the phone cuts off.

I hold back the tears.
From now on, it'll be easier
to bury what **I'm feeling**.

I'm feeling half asleep.
I've been up since 4.30,
getting in a swim before school.
As the bell goes
for registration,

Fazel walks into class
and takes his seat at the back.
I pick up my bag and
sit next to him.

I'm not trying to save you,
I'm just keeping you company
on your first day back,
that's all.

He looks at me.
I think I see a hint
of a **smile**.

268 days before

We only have enough money
for three days in the cheap hotel.
We pack our bags
and try and find a place to stay.

Tesfay marvels at the glass skyscrapers.
This is heaven, Sammy.
One day . . . One day
I'll design buildings like these.
I'll design one so tall
you can forever have your head in the stars!

We hear of a UN facility
from two Somali boys
we travelled with in the desert.

We're not far from the shiny hotels
and boulevards
when we find ourselves on narrow streets
and in dark alleyways.

We stand in front of a run-down building.
I'm hesitant to go in,
but Tesfay reminds me
that we have no other choice.

It's crammed full of people
with rows and rows of mattresses
lining the floor.

The underbelly of Tripoli.
A flipside to the touristy
glass high-rises.
Cramped and unbearable.

But we're just happy
to have a roof
over our heads.
Almost.

Almost two weeks after Fazel's attack
the police are none the wiser.

It doesn't help that I didn't see who did it.
They were wearing masks and
there was no CCTV, he says.

The three of us sit on a hill behind Dover Castle,
seagulls swooping over our heads.
Mel screams as one gets too close to her chips.

Dover is beautiful.

I wouldn't go that far, Faze, she laughs.

I heard you punched Kevin Smith.
I know you didn't do it for me,
but I've wanted to do that for so long.

He had it coming, she says
and puts an arm round him.
*And I'd do it again if you wanted me **to**.*

Together me and Tesfay
survive this hellhole,
reminding each other of home,
of our dreams.

Someone has a radio
and we listen to the football,
Manchester United versus Real Madrid.
Tesfay yells **every time Man U score**.

Every time Man U score,
there's an eruption of
yells from the lounge.

I text Mel and Fazel.
You two fancy doing something tonight?
I need to escape this house.

Fazel: I need to finish my photography coursework.

Mel: Finish it here. Mum and Dad are out. I'm lonely.

Fazel: OK.

Nat: Cool.

Mel: Great, I'll put a pizza in the oven.

Before I leave the house,
I watch Danny with Ryan in the lounge,
beers in hand,
his arm round Ryan's neck,
singing and swaying in unison
as **Man U is victorious**.

Man U is victorious.
The room erupts in cheers.
For a moment,
we forget where we are
and it is **glorious**.

266 days before

Tesfay and I stare out at the sea.
We'll be in a boat, making this crossing, soon enough.
I can't wait to get out of here.
My body can't take any more beatings,
Tesfay says, examining the bruises on his torso.

Talking of beatings, don't look now, I say,
but there's a gang approaching.

Same ones as before? Tesfay's voice trembles.

I think so . . .

Hey! You two! the leader of the pack shouts.
Dirty cockroaches like you don't belong on this beach.

Tesfay and I are frozen,
wishing the sand would
swallow us whole.

You look at me when I talk to you, cockroach!

Leave us alone! We're not doing anything!
screams Tesfay.

Oh, the little slave boy has found his voice.
Maybe I should've cut out your tongue
when I kicked the shit out of you yesterday.

Please, I say. *We haven't done anything.*

You trespass on our beach,
you look at our sea,
you walk our pavements –
fifty dollars for your crimes.

It's not a crime!
And we don't have
that sort of money! shouts Tesfay.

Fifty dollars or we kick the shit out of you.

Tesfay and I close our eyes
and take **a beating**.

> **A beating** is what she needs, fucking refugee lover.
>> Get a life.
>> UR mother must be so proud, picking on a schoolgirl.

My heart sinks reading comments
on the Facebook page.

> U shld be ashamed. People here need help.
>> Another bot.
>> YOU should be ashamed.
>
> Well done, you go, girl!
>
> So proud of you – keep going! Have donated.
>
> I'm in awe!!
>
> I hope you drown in the Channel.
>> Seriously?
>> That's dark. You need help.
>> Just cos u don't agree u don't wish death on someone.
>
> Why do you hate your country?
>> Why do you hate innocent humans who need help?
>
> You are AMAZING. Just donated!
>
> Good British men are being killed because of these terrorists.
> How can you live with yourself?

> Refugees are not terrorists.
> Ignore him. Sickos!

Don't read them, Nat. They're sick in the head.

This is awful, Mel! Why would someone write something like that?

You can't try and understand trolls, babe. That's why they're called trolls.

I keep scrolling until
Mel takes my phone away.

I told you not to look.

Give it back.

No, I told you not to look.

Don't boss me around.

I'm not . . .

Yes you are! You always do!

What?
Her voice small.

I keep going.
You do. It's like you think I'm stupid.
You think because you've got a big house and loads of expensive shit
that you know better, but you don't.
You actually haven't got a clue about the real world!

Nat . . .

Why are you even with me?
You trying to slum it or something?

The colour drains from Mel's face
and she swallows back tears.
Look at the donations that have come in.
Her voice breaking.
You've got £558 in two weeks – that's huge.
And look at the lovely comments.
I just think you're brilliant and brave and amazing,
that's why I'm with you.

And then she bursts out crying.

I'm sorry. I'm sorry, I say.
Over and **over**.

261 days before

There's a film crew
in the building today
wanting interviews,
shoving cameras in our faces.
We are asked by translators
if we want to give statements.

These arseholes come every few weeks,
a young Somali man called Bashir moans.
Different countries,
different TV stations,
saying the same thing.
'We want to inform the people, so you can get help.'
It's bullshit.
Nothing changes.

> *Baba, how can you write your articles?*
> *Aren't you afraid?*

> *You have to live fearlessly, Sammy.*
> *Use your voice to tell the truth.*
> *You cannot live your life being afraid.*

I cover my face with a scarf.
I can speak English, I say.

Get him miked! shouts a tall white man.
Another white man,
shorter and rounder than the one giving orders,
clips a microphone to my T-shirt
and shines a bright light on to my face.

How long have you been here?
the interviewer asks.

Almost two weeks, I reply.

What has your experience been so far?

Terrible.

In what way terrible? Can you explain?

I quickly try and collect my thoughts
and remain calm at the same time.
My throat feels dry
and sweat trickles down my temples.

I've seen so much death.
I've nearly starved to death.
It's not safe on the streets here.
We are beaten daily.

What country are you from?

I don't want to say which country because I fear for my family who remain.

Is that why you left?

Yes. My father was murdered.
There's forced conscription.
It's slavery.

Is there a particular country you're aiming for?

The UK.

Why the UK?

I have family there.
I hear it's safe.
Land of the free.

The man looks at me
like he knows something
I don't.

What are conditions like here?

It's overcrowded as you can see.
It's not safe. Especially for women.
There's also disease.
I want to leave.

Why don't you?

I'm scared to leave,
but I'm also scared to stay.

. . . **but I'm also scared to stay.**

I'm transfixed by the news report.
His face half covered with a scarf,
a band of dark skin
and the most striking eyes
I've ever
seen.

257 days before

Get on, he says,
opening the door of the truck.
Bodies
crammed in tight,
squinting
into the light.

We were told it would be a vehicle for five.

Our smuggler laughs.
What can I say?
Get in or get lost.

Tesfay and I
climb in
and
over bodies.

This is it, brother, says Tesfay.
We're nearly in Europe.

I dread thinking about
the crossing,
the sea.
I close my eyes and
all I see is
the water.

The water temperature is dropping.
It's November,
but I keep training in the sea to
build up my tolerance to the cold.

Fazel sits with Mel

as she films my session
for social media.
It helps with the sponsorship, she says.
Although it also feeds the trolls.
Apparently, I am also too ugly to swim the Channel.
We laughed at that one.

Fazel takes photos
while Dad records my times
and watches my technique.
It feels like I have my
very own squad.

Get on with it! shouts Dad.

I swim,
thinking of the boy on the TV,
his eyes,
his pain
and how much he's lost.

I can't get him out of my head.
With every stroke, I feel
some sort of connection to him.
I swim faster,
trying to shake off the weird feeling,
and head back to **the beach**.

The beach! says a woman.
They haven't tricked us.

I wipe away dirt from the window
and **we stare out at the sea**.

We stare out at the sea,
sipping hot chocolate.
I wince every time I lift the cup to my lips.

My whole body aches,
but my shoulders and arms feel it the most.
It's like I've done ten rounds in a boxing match.
I take a deep breath of cold, fresh sea air.
Despite the pain,
I've never felt better.

Mel scrolls through Fazel's photos.
You're really good, Faze.

Thank you. I was taught by my dad.
He was a professional photographer.

Like political stuff? she asks.

No, he laughs. *Nothing like that.*
Weddings mainly.
I'd go with him.
It was cool
capturing the happiest day of people's lives.

Is that what you want to do as a career? I ask.

Yes. If I can, I'd like to.
Maybe more street photography.
I like catching unexpected moments – they're more real, I think . . .
You know . . . I read your Facebook, Natalie.
I didn't know about your mother. That she died . . .
I recognize her.
She was my friend's caseworker.
He said she was a really good person . . .
I'm so sorry for your loss.

Thank you.
I choke back tears.
You've lost so much more. I can't even imagine.

Loss is loss, Natalie.
A family can be one person or many people.

This we share.
I'm sorry I called you a white saviour.

You don't need to apologize.
Maybe I am – was – trying to be.
I dunno. Maybe I was trying to balance stuff out.
Right some wrongs.

What do you mean?

How can I even begin to tell Fazel
about **my brother**?

My brother.
Tesfay's face lights up.
We're so close! he says.

We wait in a makeshift house
with other refugees,
all of whom have seen death in the Sahara,
all fleeing war and famine.

But to smugglers
we're a price per head,
dead or alive.
Tesfay and I find a corner
to call our own.

Tomorrow we'll be so close to paradise.
Tesfay's optimism has rarely waned.
But for me
something is stirring.
An unease . . .

An unease creeps
under my skin.

I look at my phone
and see a string of messages.

Mel: OMG, EDL march in Dover this weekend.
          Sickos!

Fazel: What's EDL?

Mel: English Defence League.
          Bunch of racists. Stay indoors on Saturday!

Fazel: Really?

Mel: Yeah, it won't be safe.
          What's happening to the world?

Nat: Just seen on Facebook there's a counter-protest.
          Look on WE LOVE DOVER page.

Mel: You're not thinking of going, are you?

Nat: Why not? We have to stand up to these people.
          We can't let them win. Complicit in silence,
          remember.

Mel: You're right. Oh God, I'm scared, but OK.

Fazel: Me too. The right to protest is a privilege.
          I'll be **there**.

256 days before

We're taken to the coast.
There are already a hundred refugees
being loaded on to a boat.
In a panic we rush towards it,
stumbling,
falling,
clambering
over one another.
Men with rifles strike us
and hold us back
as we watch our boat fill with people
and sail away.

That was our boat! we shout.
That was our boat!!!

A riot erupts on the beach.
Some people jump in the sea
and try to swim after it.
Others say, *There must be a second boat.*

But there isn't.
There was only one
and it left without us
already **full**.

Full of
confusion
despair
hate
love.

Not
sleeping –

tossing
turning
fighting
to
       stay
           afloat.

Ryan, talk to me.
Ryan!
Why won't you talk?
My hands on his face,
trying to prise his mouth open.
It's stuck.
I punch and kick.
Nothing moves him.
Danny is there.
I shout but no words come out.
I'm punching and kicking.
Ryan, Ryan!

Another zombie day,
another sleepless night.
Body aching,
shoulders burning,
legs cramping,
the chafing under my armpits
becoming
unbearable.

I look in on Ryan before I leave for school.
He's buried under his duvet,
his rose-tattooed arm hanging loose,
knuckles scraping the carpet.

A stack of leaflets on his desk catches my eye.
LET'S GET OUR COUNTRY BACK
with an EDL logo in the corner.

My heart's beating out of my chest.

My heart's beating out of my chest.
I put my head in my hands
and sob silently.

Do I love?
Do I feel?
Am I even human?

I don't know.

I
don't
know.

I don't know how to tell you this, Dad, but . . .

I give him the leaflet.
I tell him everything.
I make him listen.

He sits down.
He takes it in.
He buries his face in his **hands**.

255 days before

The morning sun rises
in the makeshift house.

I wake to bodies splintering wood
with the weight of their hanging.
This is what becomes of **pain**.

Pain, Dad. Here. In my chest. Every day.
It feels like everything's been taken away from us.

There are no excuses, Ryan.
I'm not having this sort of muck in my house.

Dad holds out the EDL leaflet,
scrunches it up
and tosses it in the bin.

Aren't you angry?
We can't find a place to live cos of them.

Them who? What you on about?

You don't see it, Dad.

You've lost me, Ryan. I ain't got a clue what to say to you.

You make me feel useless, you know that? he shouts.

How do I?

Ryan bites his bottom lip.
You don't see it. You're too busy with Nat.

I'm still here for you.

Yeah, right. She can do no wrong and I'm a piece of shit.

You've got it wrong, Ryan.

I don't need either of you. I'm moving out.
Danny says I can stay with him . . .

Who's Danny?

My mate, Dad.
He's actually been there for me,
which is more than I can say for you.

You can't move out, Ryan.
This is your home.

Well, I'm not wanted here.
Danny says he can help me find work.

Where? What kind of work?

Just stuff. I'm not changing my mind.
I'm done.

Then he walks out of the house,
leaving the door swinging behind **him**.

254 days before

We're taken once again
to the shore
in the middle of the night.

It's dark when we arrive.
I try and soak in the moon's light,
help my eyes to see.

I can hear the waves
lapping at the shore.
I think I can even see the
froth of white as they crash,
but I can't see a boat.

Where's the boat?

Ahead, says a man.

I can't see it, says Tesfay.

He gestures out towards the sea.
My eyes adjust.

A dinghy? But we were promised a ship, I say.
We were shown pictures of cruise ships.

He laughs.

We paid for a ship, adds Tesfay.

He shrugs.
Get in or stay – your choice.

Get in or stay.
Get in or we leave you.

Get in or we beat you.
Get in or . . .
is all we hear.

Choiceless
voiceless
hopeless
helpless.

There are seventy of us.
Seventy bodies to fit
in this rubber boat.

We are marched in single file and
loaded on to the dinghy,
packed in like sardines.

I feel the bottom bow
with all our weight as
more two-thousand-dollar bodies pile on.

The dinghy is packed to absolute capacity.
We sit in a tangle of limbs.
I'm thrown a small bottle of water.
Tesfay and I sit side by side,
not looking at each other.
It's best not to witness
the terror in each other's eyes.

It's the dead of night,
less chance of being spotted
as we sail across a body of water known
for more sinkings and storms than any other.
We are at its mercy.
I pray it's not to our deaths.
The way thousands
have gone **before**.

Before, my life didn't seem
to have a purpose.
But this swim,
the training,
it's giving me something
to hold on to.

Come on, Nat, you're slower than last week.
Pick up your pace.

I am exhausted
and the raw skin under my arms stings.

I look at Dad.
He's got a new lease of life training me.
I see how much it means to him.

I take three gulps of an energy drink,
rotate my arms,
stretch my legs
and jump into the pool,
ready to go again.

I check the time.
I'm not even halfway through the session
yet it feels like I've been training **for hours**.

For hours we float,
having no idea which direction we go in.
Tesfay and I hold on to each other
as the dinghy rocks back and forth.

I look up at the night sky.
The stars are bigger and brighter
than I've ever seen before.

I look up at the night sky.

**The stars are bigger and brighter
than I've ever seen before.**
I'm hanging with half my body out of the window
when I see **two shooting stars fly across the sky**.

Two shooting stars fly across the sky
and everyone starts clapping.
I laugh out loud.

> **I laugh out loud.**
> I've never seen shooting stars before.
> Maybe **it's a good sign** . . .

It's a good sign! I say.

Yes it is, says Tesfay
as we hold each other's trembling bodies.

Better days ahead.

> . . . **Better days ahead,**
> **I hope**.

I hope so, he says.

> *Look, Baba, two shooting stars!*
> *If one catches the other, will they explode?*
>
> *No. They are just pieces of rock that will fall to earth.*
>
> *Do stars catch up with each other eventually?*
>
> *There are binary stars that orbit each other from birth.*

What happens to them?

Eventually, they **join**.

253 days before

The waves pick up.
The boat sways and rocks.
Menacing dark-grey clouds
rage across a starless sky.

Bodies pressed against bodies,
holding on for our lives,
as rain pours down on us.
It's icy cold.

It's icy cold.
I nestle into my Dryrobe
and drink my hot chocolate.
The sun disappears behind dark clouds.
The waves get bigger and
the wind picks up,
rain pelting down.
I look out at the raging sea,
grateful I made it out in **time**.

252 days before

It's early morning.

It's early morning.

Morning sun rises.
We battled waves all night.

All night I've tossed and turned.

Tossed and turned as the wind howls.
Only God can save us, says a man.

A man talks about the EDL march
on breakfast TV,
my stomach in knots.

My stomach in knots
as we notice
water coming in,
only a trickle.

A trickle of people all
walking in the same direction.
Dover is quiet, eerie.
I see police barricades and
my heart feels like it's beating
one thousand times a minute.

My heart feels like it's beating
one thousand times a minute.
We try and find the leak,
but it's impossible.
Every square inch is crammed with **people**.

> **People**,
> hundreds of them,
> on **both sides**.

Both sides of the boat
start to bow out,
like it's splitting in **two**.

> **Two** police officers try and hold back
> an angry mob.
> More bodies gather.
> **A baby is crying.**
> **I want to vomit.**

A baby is crying.
I want to vomit as
the wind picks up
and the boat rocks violently.
The sky splits with
a deafening rumble.

> **A deafening rumble**
> that increases in volume
> as a crowd of people comes towards us.
> **I can hear my heartbeat in my ears,**
> **like a drum.**

I can hear my heartbeat in my ears,
like a drum.
There's chaos in the dinghy
as we feel ourselves getting tossed around
by a force bigger than we can imagine.
We are carried
we are thrown
we cling on
we scream
we cry
we pray
we beg
we fight.

We fight.
Peaceful protest turns ugly
in the blink of an eye.

The EDL hurl insults at us and
we spit back.
The police keep us separated.
Then
I see him.
He sees me.
Ryan.
Me and Ryan.
Opposite sides.
I feel myself sink.

I feel myself sink into the sea
as water fills the boat,
and no sooner do we scoop it out
than more pours in.
A battle.

A battle.
Glass bottles are thrown,
police try and hold back the throbbing crowd of
EDL on one side
and anti-racists on the other.
Both sides are angry,
pushing and shoving.
It's chaos.

It's chaos.
The waves crash over us,
turning the ink-black sea orange
as people are **thrown**.

      Thrown to the ground
      as both sides merge,
      creating one angry mass.
      I struggle to get up.
      Ryan! I shout.
      But he doesn't hear **me**.

Me and Tesfay, we cling on to the boat
as people are thrown into the sea,
they scream and yell for **help**.

      Help! *Ryan!* I shout out to him again,
      but there are too many **people**.

People all around me as
I'm flung from the dinghy.
Tesfay!
A huge wave comes crashing over me.
I see him
clinging on to the boat
on the other side.

On the other side
I finally see him.
Just when I manage to stand,
there's a huge wave of people.
I am pushed,
taken by the wave . . .

I am pushed,
taken by the wave.
I sink

       I sink

I come up

       I come up

I come up
fight for breath
I sink
I come up . . .

       I come up
       fight for breath
       I sink
       I come up.

I come up.
Waves bigger than I have ever seen.
By a miracle, I grab hold of the dinghy.
We're taken back and forth,
thrown up and down,
as **the storm rages.**

The storm rages.
I watch Ryan make waves through the crowd,
as these angry people
are pushing me down.
I'm
losing where I am.

I'm
losing where I am.
I'm thrown up and down.
Tired and cold.
Tesfay, I hear Tesfay.
I turn my body in the water,
I see him.
Tesfay!
I see him.
Fighting.

I see him.
Fighting.
Ryan!
I see him fighting
and then he disappears.
Ryan!!!!!!

I see him fighting
and then he disappears.
Tesfay!!!!!!
Tesfay, who saved me in the desert,
disappears into the sea.

I am in
the sea
in a sea of
orange
arms and legs

fish with no gills
but mouths open
gasping
reaching
eyes
searching
waves crashing
over our
bodies.

        Bodies
        in a sea of red.
        Red faces,
        angry
        and helpless.
        The sound,
        the roar
        like nothing I've heard before.
        Waves of people crashing and crushing,
        shouting and running.
        A sound like gunshot echoes in our ears.
        We scream
        and scatter.
        I see Ryan . . .
        I run I run I run.

I swim I swim I swim.

        I run I run I run.

I swim I swim I swim.
I dive under,
try and search for Tesfay.

Try and search for Ryan,
try and catch up with him.

Tesfay!   Ryan!

                In a sea of bodies.

In a sea of bodies
I come up
and go down
again and again and again,
searching for hope.
Tesfay!

                        Ryan!
                        I can't lose him!
                        I can't!

I can't lose him!
I can't!
I keep diving and searching.
I can't see anything.
Exhausted,
I think of drawing my last breath
when I'm blinded by **bright lights**.

                        Bright lights and sirens.
                        I'm dazed and confused.

I'm dazed and confused.
A boat. A real boat.
I can't believe it.

I can't believe it.
How did this happen?
I'm in a crowd of people,
running, screaming.
It's hard to make sense of anything.
I'm crouched on the ground,
everywhere a sea of feet,
until **a hand reaches out** . . .

A hand reaches out.
I grab hold, and am instantly blinded by
a bright flash in my eyes.

A bright flash in my eyes
from Fazel's camera.
Mel grabs my hand and lifts me up.

Oh my God, Nat, thank God.
We've been looking for you everywhere.
You're not hurt, are you?

Nothing serious.

It's not safe, Nat.
Come on, let's get out of here.

I hold on to both Mel and Fazel
as they carry **my bruised body**.

My bruised body
is pulled and lifted on to a vessel.
I retch up my guts.
I fall on the floor.
I slip and slide with the waves.
I am held.
I am helped.

I am wrapped up in a blanket.
I am spoken to in languages I do not understand,
but looked at with eyes I do.
They are eyes similar to Baba's
and they tell me I am **safe**.

Tesfay
the footballer

the joker

the son

my heart

was, you'd love him.

like I did, like he

if you knew him

my brother   my friend

Ryan
the footballer

the joker

the son

my heart

was, you'd love him.

like I did, like he

if you knew him

my brother   my friend

179

TESFAY ABEL SOLOMON

18.6.2000 – 10.11.2018

I lie half on another body.
I can barely move.
The body next to me shakes,
or maybe it's mine?

Men with white masks
and plastic gloves
shout instructions.

The cold is unbearable,
a silver blanket
the only barrier against the icy winds.

I can't move.
I feel nothing.
Why him and not me?
He was the brave one.
He deserved to live.

We rock gently on the rescue boat.
Everyone silent,
mourning all the lives
that have been lost.

> *Whatever happens, Sammy,*
> *do not forget*
> *how to love,*
> *your worth,*
> *who you are,*
> *how to feel.*
> *Keep checking,*
> *because when you see awful sights –*
> *and you will –*
> *these are the things that are easy to forget.*

I search
deep inside myself.
No.

No, I don't think I do.
I am completely empty inside.

I am completely empty inside.
I find clips of the protest-turned-riot on YouTube.
Hundreds have been uploaded and
I watch them over and over.
Angry men and women,
some with their kids,
carrying placards
with slogans
based on
lies
and
hate.

Mel's mum hovers over me and
puts a hand on my shoulder.
She shakes her head.

I think that's enough for now, Natalie.
It can't be good for you to keep watching those videos.

But I'm obsessed.
Searching for Ryan in the chaos.
Going through each video
one by one.

One by one
we're taken off the boat,
lined up,
given a number to hold and
made to have our photo taken.

Which country? the man behind the desk asks.

Eritrea, I say.

We take our silver blankets
and sit in large rooms.
One man starts preaching.
Families huddle together
and repeat the gospel after him.

Do I have faith?
I search for the answer.
No.
Not when the sea took Tesfay
and left **me**.

Me and Mel, we
sit cuddled up on the sofa.
We don't talk –
she just holds me
as **I try and figure out a way
forward with this
black cloud hanging over me.**

**I try and figure out a way
forward with this
black cloud hanging over me.**
I sit outside the centre,
rows and rows of men, women and children
all huddled in their silver blankets
like the stars have fallen from the sky
and landed right here in Lampedusa.

I hear shouting from the yard.
Eritrea, Syria, Sudan, Iraq!
I go to see what's happening.
A fight at a time like this?

A whistle is blown
and my body relaxes

as a group of young men and boys
start kicking a deflated ball.
It's Syria versus Eritrea
– first round.

There is chanting
and clapping
like at a real football match.
Syria scores the first goal
and half the spectators rejoice
while the other half fake-commiserates.
Chants of *Er-ree-tray-aa*
and *Sy-ree-aa* fill the yard.

Tesfay was a great footballer,
so quick and nimble.
I imagine him here
playing, scoring a goal.
It feels too painful
to participate.
I leave the yard
and find a place
to sit by myself.

I always thought Tesfay and I
were binary stars.
Forever in each other's orbit since birth.
Why didn't the sea take me?
Then we'd be joined once more.

There's a hand on my shoulder.
Brother,
someone says.
I turn round;
I can't believe my eyes.

Hamid.

250 days before

I can't sleep.
I can't stay awake.
I'm forever in
an in-between state.

7 a.m.
Monday.
Another training session
before school.

It's feeling harder.
I slip on my swimming costume,
pack my goggles and hat
and head down to the beach.

Pebbles glisten
in the morning sun,
as waves gently ebb and flow
from the shoreline.

A gentle icy breeze
numbs my skin
before I'm even in the water.

Dad has a cash-in-hand job
helping with an extension.
I'm alone today.

The water is calm,
a gentle ripple.
Today France is clear.

I wave.
I don't know why.
I always do this,

wonder if anyone is waving back.
Makes me feel less alone.

Yesterday's winds
leaving the sea brown and muddy
at the shore, with its ink-blackness
further out.

I close my eyes,
let the water lap at my feet,
feel the pebbles dig into my soft skin.

It's twelve degrees in the water.
The sleepiness starts to lift
as the cold seeps in.

I swim quickly,
trying to warm myself up.
But I feel heavy,

my body lagging behind
with its extra layer of baggage.
It's exactly four months today.

Grief comes in waves, they say.
You have to ride the storms.
Today I'm swimming in a storm
as my goggles fill with **tears**.

Tears stream down my face as
I tell Hamid about Tesfay.
How I tried to save him
and how I don't know how I'll ever
be able to tell his mother or forgive myself.

Hamid tells me about Petros and Yonas.
We were all together to Benghazi.
We travelled to the shore

and then we were separated, put on different boats.
We were in sight of each other for a night and a day,
but after the second night,
when the sun came up,
their boat was nowhere to be seen.

What happened to it?

I don't want to think about it.

I don't want to think about it any more.
Ryan is consuming my every thought.
I'm so tired.

I'm curled up on Mel's bed.

You need to forget about Ryan –
he's not your problem . . .

It is my problem.
He's my brother, Mel.

I know that. But you can't change him.
Focus on the swim and the talent contest.

She pulls out a fifties-style prom dress from her wardrobe.
It's just like the one Taylor Swift wears in her video.
What do you think?

I don't care, Mel!
Are you even listening to me?
Dad's got his head in the sand –
he won't even talk about Ryan.
All you care about is your stupid costume . . .

Yeah, a stupid costume for a talent contest
raising money for your swim.
Sorry for trying to help.

I know, I know. Sorry.
It's just . . .
My head's a mess.

Talk to me, Nat.
I'm here.
I'm always gonna be here.
Just stop pushing me away.

I know, I'm sorry.

Look, I realize this is a little off topic,
but I've got some big news.

What?

Well, I started thinking,
we've got to think bigger
if we're gonna raise
five thousand pounds by next July.
So I got Mum to make a few calls.
There's a woman in her Pilates class
who works in PR.

So?

So . . . how do you feel about
doing an interview for the local paper?

For real?

For real!
We've got to try everything and you,
my little warrior queen,
*have to keep **fighting**.*

Fighting breaks out round the telephone booths.
So many wanting to call home.

I try and block out the noise and dial.
It's a while before anyone picks up.

Mama?

Sammy, Sammy, you're alive!
Where are you now?

Italy. On an island.

You made it.
Oh thank God!
How is Tesfay?
His mama's worried sick.

I can't find the words.

What is it, Sammy?

The sea took him, Mama.

She's silent.

I tried, I tried to save him.
You must believe me.

I believe you, Sammy.

I'll tell Tesfay's family.
They need to hear it from me.

My phone card runs out and
another eager young man
takes my place,
frantically dialling,
needing to tell a loved one
he's safe.

Hamid puts an arm round me.
I lost my brother, Hamid, I sob.

It's you and me now, he says.

He puts out his hand
and places mine on top.

*Go alone and go fast or
go together and go far.
Together,* he says.

And in losing one brother
I gain **another**.

Another newspaper
showing photos of the protest-turned-riot.
I turn the pages.
A lottery win
ads for a sofa sale
a lost dog
a cheating husband
a corrupt councillor
a closed library
homelessness rising
a women's shelter closing
funding cuts
evictions and

on page twenty-two
I see him.
The boy from the news report
on the TV.
Those same eyes,
barely keeping his head above water,
being pulled out of the sea,
staring right at me
like he knows me,
like I know **him**.

243 days before

A brick thrown
– a window smashed
– owners terrorized.

CCTV shows
– an Asian couple hiding
– thugs wearing masks
– a shop being wrecked.

Masks can't hide a person
– when you know how they stand
– how they run
– the ink on their skin.

You don't need to see a face
to know who **someone is**.

Someone is screaming.
Not another boat!
I can't get on another boat!
Please no!
I'd rather die!
I'd rather die!

My hysteria
stays locked
inside.

My legs shake
as I board the boat.
Vomit rises
from my stomach.

Where are we going?
I ask a man.

Detention centre –
They take us from one hell to the next.

Jump off the boat, I think.
Join Tesfay under the waves.
> Keep going, keep going, keep going.
> For Tesfay, for Tesfay, for Tesfay.

My two voices.

My two voices:
I should say something
> *but he's my brother*
doesn't matter
> *but no one was hurt*
that's not the point.
> *It's just a broken window.*
> *It was just glass,*
> *just **broken glass**.*

Broken glass
scattered across the ground,
bins overflow,
rats feed off rubbish,
bare concrete and metal,
a barbed-wire fortress.

Hamid and I share a metal container
with ten other boys,
threadbare mattresses on the floor
and holes in the rusted metal walls.
We breathe and freeze
as **winter sinks its teeth in**.

Winter sinks its teeth in.
I fight the cold,
training harder.

The harder I train,
**the further I push
the guilt
of what
I know
away**.

**The further I push
the guilt
of what
I know
away,
the
worse
I
feel.**
Guilt eats
away at me.

I call Tesfay's mother.
I'm sorry, I say. I tried to save him.

But you didn't, she says. You didn't.

I know, I say. I know.
I wish he was still here.

I wish he was still here.
I wish he hadn't moved out.
I wish Mum was alive –
he wouldn't have changed.
I know it.
I know it in my heart.

I train every day.
When Dad tells me I need to rest,
I ignore him.
Focusing on the Channel swim
will make all the
ugly go   away.

Then I sit in a
class with Fazel
and I can't look
him in the **eye**.

242 days before

At school
I see Year Seven kids whispering,
That's her! and nudging each other.
A new-found fame.
I'm not used to being so visible.

Mel loves it.
We're queens of the school, she says,
just in time for Kevin Smith to push past us,
holding his nose.

Something smells like rotten fish!

I miss **being invisible**.

Being invisible
is an advantage in this hellhole
as Hamid and I talk about escaping.
We spend our time trying to keep warm
in a rusted metal room.
We haven't washed in days.
Someone cut their wrists,
they'd had enough, and
no one's cleaned up the mess
in the showers **yet**.

238 days before

The boy with the brown eyes,
I know him.

Sounds stupid, I know,
but it's true.

It's like we're connected.
It's like I feel his pain,

which is ridiculous.
I haven't been through

what he's been through.
But once you know loss and pain

you see it in others.
You can feel it in all its rawness.

No matter who you are,
or where you're from,

that pain
it's all of ours

and once you experience it
there's no going back.

I am swimming.
I am drowning.
Waves crashing,
I hold out my hand,
but
I sink.
I wake from my nightmare . . .

I am swimming.
I am drowning.
Waves crashing,
I hold out my hand,
but
I sink.
I wake from my nightmare
sweaty,
panting,
thankful that
it was just a dream.

I can't sleep.
I leave my cold container
and step outside.
It's freezing.
I rub my hands together
and hunch up my shoulders.

Then, out of nowhere,
a group of ten men
throw their blankets over
the barbed wire
and take a running jump
over the fence.
I hear their bodies land on the ground.
I hear moans and cries.
Then I see them escape
into the **darkness**.

225 days before

Ryan's home.
Walks in, puts his bag down.
What's for tea? he asks,
like he's never been away,
like nothing's happened.

Dad gives him a hug.
It's good to have you back, son.

Dad thinks he's turned a corner.
Told you it was just a phase, Nat.
He's convinced. I'm not so sure.
I check his phone.

> don't say nothing. keep ur head down. D

We get a call from the housing office.
We move in two weeks –
a two-bed –
we can take it or leave it.
Dad looks at Ryan, at me.
We can make it work, he says.

I'm not quite with it
when I have my interview
with the *Dover Express*.
Mel's sitting next to me,
more excited than I am.
My thoughts are elsewhere.
Ryan . . . moving . . .
my head begins to pound.

The journalist looks at me sympathetically.
It must be exhausting, juggling school with all that swimming.

Yeah it is, I say.

I tell her how often I train,
that wetsuits aren't allowed,
how cold the sea is now,
how long it might take me,
and when and how I lost my mum.

She sighs and 'wows' and looks sad
in all the right places
and tells me how brave I am.

I am not brave
I am not brave
I am not brave.

I can't even look at myself
in the mirror
any more.

I swallow my guilt and shame.
I haven't told Mel or Dad
that Ryan is responsible
for terrorizing the couple in the shop,
that he smashed their window
and graffitied racist words on the wall.
I haven't told anyone, and
it's weighing down on me
like a pile of bricks.

I'm a coward.
I'm not **brave**.

Brave. I must be brave.
We don't eat our one meal.
We keep it, hide it, save it,
in our bags.

In the dead of night
we take our blankets

and do exactly as I saw the men doing
a few nights before.

We throw our blankets over the barbed wire
and start to climb up.
The wire pokes holes
in the blanket and tears it
and the spikes dig into my hands.

I collapse back on to the ground in pain.
Hamid tries and falls back down,
his hands bleeding.

We have to get out, Hamid.
We have to keep trying.

My legs, arms and hands
are scratched to pieces
and my ankle twists as I land.

I bite my arm to stop from screaming
and stumble into the night
with Hamid at my side.

We don't know
where we're going.
We limp and drag ourselves
through wasteland
until we can't go any further.

We wrap our jackets round us.
It's so cold, but
we dare not sleep,
frightened we might never
wake **up**.

222 days before

Dad and I go to see the flat.

It's this or nothing, he says.

It smells damp.

I can fix it up, Nat.

With what?

Well, I've got that job working on the houses
on the new Prospect estate.
That should keep us going for a bit.

We're on the other side of town, Dad.
Miles away from the beach, school, friends.

There's a bus stop at the top of the hill.

Where are we gonna sleep?

I'll take the couch. You and Ryan take the bedrooms.

You're basically in the kitchen, Dad.

It's fine, love. I'll make it work.
We've got a roof over our heads.
That's what matters,
not where **we sleep**.

We sleep in parks.
The cold is fierce,
angry
and bitter.

I wrap my jacket tight round me,
but it's so thin.
A jacket for the summer
not the middle of winter.
My hands and feet are
blocks of ice.

Every night a group of people
set up tables,
pour soup into bowls,
give us bread rolls
and hot cups of tea.
Hamid and I line up
with other men and women
who sleep in doorways,
under bridges
and on park benches like us.

An Eritrean woman
tells us about a shelter we
can go to during the day.
There's hot food
and a place to shower.
Hamid and I can't believe our ears.
It sounds like a Utopia.

Come by tomorrow, she says.
There are other Eritreans.
Hamid and I walk over to our bench,
excited about this magical place
we'll visit tomorrow.

From where we sit, we can see
the Christmas tree in Turin.
It's like nothing I have ever seen before.
It's huge.
So many lights,
it could power an entire village in Eritrea.

I feel like there's more love for this tree
than for us humans.

I want to climb inside it.
I want to feel the warmth of its branches.
I want people to see me like they see this tree.
All lights and **love**.

211 days before

Moving day,
four days before Christmas.
I take my last midnight walk round our house.
I'm a mess.
Losing this house
is like losing Mum all over again.
My heart
fuck me
my heart.

My heart
breaks every time I talk to Mama.
It takes all my strength to keep up the lie.
I'm not the only one who does it –
you hear it in every phone call,
the lies
we tell our loved ones,
that all the money
and worry was worth **it**.

It's on the fifth floor,
I tell Mel and Fazel,
who have come
to help us move.

There's a lift, right? asks Mel.

Yeah, I think so.

Good.

Fazel presses the button for the lift
as a young woman struggles with a pram
down the stairs.

It's broken! she shouts
and then looks at our boxes.
Where you moving?

Fifth floor, I say.

Oh God, she says. *Good **luck**.*

207 days before

Are you coming home for Christmas dinner, Ry?

Ryan left this morning after opening his presents.
Said he was going out for fags –
that was six hours ago.

Ryan is typing,
        then the dots disappear.
I wait.
See if they come back.
They don't.

Where the hell has Ryan got to?

Dunno, Dad. I'll put the veg in the oven.
I don't think Ryan's **coming**.

Coming to the soup kitchen
has given Hamid and me a family of sorts.
There's tea and biscuits
and one hot meal a day.
Today it's Christmas.
The tables are full, with meats, vegetables and pasta,
stretching from one end of the room to the other,
and we wear paper hats that look like crowns
and have whistles that sound like trumpets.
We each choose a little gift from a bag.
Hamid gets a box of chocolates
and I get **a key ring**.

A key ring *– what did you get, Dad?*

Lip balm. Wanna trade?

We swap our Christmas-cracker gifts,
trying to hide how we're really feeling.
First Christmas without Mum,
and first Christmas without Ryan.

Look at this place.
We haven't even got any decorations up.

Who needs a tree, Dad?
I'm here with you – that's all that matters to me.

I just . . . I just wish your mum was here, you know?

I reach across the table
and hold his hand.
Yeah. I know. Me too.

We look through old photos
and watch videos of her,
and Dad cries a bit more
and drinks a little too much
and falls asleep on the sofa.

I see Mel in the evening.
They've got a Christmas tree that's eight feet tall.
They need one that big because of the high ceilings
(any smaller wouldn't look right)
and they play party games
like a real family.

For one night,
I forget
I choose to forget.

For one night,
I forget
I choose to forget
as an old man plays his guitar

and we sing songs
and dance to pop music.
Buon Natale! we say over and over.
This is the Europe I dreamed of.
This is the Europe I knew **existed**.

201 days before

Tomorrow is New Year's Day.
A new beginning.
From Turin, Hamid and I take our chance
on a tip-off from Yusef,
a man from the shelter.
There's a lay-by thirty minutes outside the city.
Lorry drivers go there to sleep on the way to Calais.
You could easily slip into a truck, he told us.

We hide in the bushes until
we notice a man leave his truck.
He walks down alongside the lay-by
to take a piss.
This is our chance.
We open the back door of the lorry
and hide in between some boxes.
We sit for almost twelve hours,
unable to move or make a sound.

When the truck is opened in Calais
and the contents unloaded,
there's nowhere for us to hide.

The driver stares at us
and we stare at the driver.
I don't know who
is more frightened.

Go, he says. *Go!*
We get out of the truck
and start running,
Wait! he shouts.

We hear his footsteps coming up behind us.
He taps me on the shoulder

and I turn round with my hands in the air.
He shoves a carrier bag into my hand.
I look inside.
It's full of food.
Now go, he says.
Go, go!

200 days before

Ten

        Nine

Eight

        Seven

Six

        Five

Four

        Three

Two

        One.

Fireworks

        explode,

the

        sky

is

        a

kaleidoscope

of

colours.

A

rainbow

of

falling

stars.

Happy

New

Year!

I love you, Mel.

Love you too, Nat.

Er, hello, what about me?

Sorry, Fazel. Get in here, group hug.

We watch the fireworks over Dover harbour.
New Year always seems so
hopeful.

So much has happened this last year.
I feel like
a completely different person.

**I feel like
a completely different person.**
I think back to a few months ago,
who I was when I left,
who I am now.

A group of us gather
to watch the fireworks
on the beach in Calais.
I turn to Hamid.
Let's make a wish.

Let's make a wish,
I say to the others.

To feel safe again, says Fazel.
Find who put me in hospital.

Rocks land in my stomach.
I've done a good job of pushing
everything I know
and suspect
to the back of my mind.

I'll second that, says Mel.

Me too, I say and
secretly make another wish.

*Don't let it be Ryan.
Please don't let it be Ryan.
Just bring him **home**.*

Home. *To just find a home,*
Hamid says.
That's it. Simple.

Mine too, I say.
We're so close.

I look up and see
the North Star,
the brightest star in the sky,
guiding us,
giving us all **hope**.

150 days before

For seven weeks,
Hamid and I wait
like jackals in the night.
We hide in the shadows,
waiting to sneak and slide under,
in and around,
find a space to call home,
to take refuge in,
before we reach
the promised land.

During the day we hide in
a disused factory,
under bridges,
under makeshift shelters,
under tents that are taken every day
and sprayed with chemicals
that make them unusable.

We have visits from volunteers
who give us food,
bring a battery pack
so we can charge our phones,
and replace our tents,
talk to us
and listen to our stories.

Anthony, an older man
with grey hair and glasses
and a belly that hangs over his jeans,
always makes time.

He pats me on the back and says,
How's it going, mate?
And, *Get that grub down you.*

Sometimes he stares into the distance
after listening to me talking
and says, *It breaks my heart, mate.*

I tell Anthony I want to practise my English
so he brings me an English newspaper called
the *Guardian.*

The Guardian, *Nat!*
You're gonna be in the Guardian!
Mel's super excited.
The money should definitely come
rolling in now.

It's the evening of the talent contest at school.
Walking into the hall,
I come face to face with Kevin.
Why are you even here? I say.

What? And miss a load of saddos
making a fool of themselves?
No chance, he says, pushing past me and
taking a seat at the back of the hall with his mates.

I sit at the front with Fazel,
prime location for him to take some photos.
I feel like a celebrity, even though I'm not performing.
I watch all the acts in awe –
I could never imagine being onstage.
I feel nervous waiting for Mel.
She's kept her act secret from me,
but I know it'll be a big dance number.
I can't imagine her shying away and
not doing a complete showstopper.

It's time, Fazel whispers.

Mel walks onstage,

no sparkly costume,
just black jeans and a plain white T-shirt.
She sits on a stool.
You could hear a pin drop it's that quiet.

She starts singing.
Her voice shakes.
No backing track,
no dancers,
just Mel
singing right at me.
For me.
We might as well
be the only two people
in the hall.

By the end of the song,
I'm crying
and everyone is out of their seats,
clapping.
A standing ovation!
We raise £867.58, taking my total to £3,000.
Mrs Edwards asks me onstage.
I'm so embarrassed, but with Mel at my side,
and looking out into the hall
with everyone cheering,
I can't quite believe the support.
It feels unreal.

Dad and I celebrate over a takeaway pizza.
Halfway through a comedy panel show,
there's a knock at the door.
It's **the police**.

The police kick and punch us,
just like the guards in Eritrea.
We're told England will be better,
but I see the headlines in the papers.

What did I leave for?
Why did Tesfay die?
For what?
For nothing.
It's the same here as it is back home.
I have nothing to live for,
nothing.
This has all been for **nothing**.

Nothing to say, Ryan?
Drugs? Really?

They let me go, didn't they?

Is that what this Danny has got you mixed up in?
Is that the 'work' he's found you?

I wasn't charged,
so what's your problem?

Don't use that tone with me, Ryan.
I know you wasn't charged,
but you're mixed up in something.
Why else would the police come round?

I'm not mixed up with anything, Dad!

I don't believe you!

They go round
in circles
like that
all night.

All night,
I look out at the white cliffs of Dover.
There's no going back.
I think of Mama's final words to me.

It's no use,
I feel nothing.
I'm just waiting
for
death.

148 days before

I read a British newspaper.
There's a girl,
one of the youngest ever,
who is training to cross
the same water
I look out on to
every day.

She's my age.
In the photo she looks
happy,
strong.
She's raising money for charity.
The charity that's here,
helping people like me.

It's weird – I can feel her close.

It's weird – I can feel him close.

I look at the article
about the refugees
being rescued at sea in Italy.
I stare at the boy
being pulled out of the water,
the same boy
from the news report on TV.
Still,

I'm drawn to his face.

I'm drawn to her **face**.

I can't seem to look away.
There's something so familiar.
I know her.
I know **her**.

146 days before

A day trip to Calais with Dad,
to volunteer with Care4Calais.

Sure we can afford this, Dad?

It was thirty quid, Nat, bloody bargain.

But still, Dad, we need the money.

I'm working, Nat.
It's not permanent, but we can spare this for now.

Dad's got some extra work
renovating a mansion
in the middle of Kent.

You should see it, Nat,
makes Mel's place look like a council house.
I'll be working there most of the year, I reckon.
You need to stop worrying.
This is important –
you have to see what you're swimming for.

When we get off the ferry,
we drive
to a warehouse
where we sort clothes.
There are people
from all over the world.
I'm told to help Gaby,
a young woman from Germany.
We sort out T-shirts
into different sizes
and Dad sorts shoes
with a lady called Reshma from Birmingham.

Gaby's in her twenties
and she's been here over a month.
I look across at Dad.
He gives me a wink and mouths,
You OK?

I nod and mouth,
Yeah!
And I really am.
For the first time
in a long time,
I really am **OK**.

OK, says Hamid,
we need to try something new.
We can't
stand in the same spot
every day
and expect things
to change.

We are huddled in our tent.
It's freezing
and my stomach grumbles
yet I don't have the energy to eat.

Maybe a lorry is not a good option.
Maybe we should get a boat?

No way, I say.

Those nights on the Mediterranean
are still anchored in my mind,
the horror of **it**.

It's been a hard morning.
At midday we drive to a nature reserve

that's being used as a camp.
I help set up the kitchen –
there's about thirty of us.

I'm freezing,
despite wearing so many layers.
I can't begin to think
what it must be like
to camp here.

As soon as we arrive,
a queue starts forming.
I serve plates of hot food.
It's non-stop for an hour,
but I don't even feel the time go by.

When it looks like everyone's been fed,
Dad and I are taken to another part of the camp
as the last few people are served.

As the last few people are served,
Hamid and I run towards the makeshift kitchen
before they pack away.
I can't believe we nearly missed our
only hot meal.
Nearly missed these people
who come with their
smiles, food,
clothes
and **conversation**.

Conversation goes a long way, says Gaby.
These people have been through so much,
they just want to be seen and heard,
to be valued.

We give out tea and biscuits
and I make myself at home
by a blue container
next to a man who says he's seventy-five
and the oldest refugee here.

He shows me his art.
Books and books of watercolours,
beautiful pictures.
This is my life, he says
and he tells me about his home
and I don't have to do any talking.
I just **listen**.

Listen, *come here –*
sit with me, Sammy.
I notice the volunteer van drive away
as I approach Abdul.
He's seventy-five,
the oldest refugee here.
He's sitting in his usual spot
by his blue container.
I saved you a biscuit, he says.

He's painting
and it amazes me
how he can still find
such bright pictures
in his mind
when my mind is getting
darker by **the day**.

The day comes to an end and
Dad and I say goodbye
to all the volunteers.
It seems as though

something has shifted inside me
and I start feeling emotional.

It's OK, says Gaby.
It can feel overwhelming.

She gives me a hug.
*I hope you come back soon – and
good luck with the swim.
I could never do something like that.*

It's nothing compared to what you all do here, I say.

Anthony, one of the volunteers,
takes a photo of us with a digital polaroid camera.
Me, Gaby, Dad and Reshma.
He prints two copies of the photo,
one for us
and one for the noticeboard,
which is covered in loads of photos.
I want to take them all in,
but Dad says we have to get back for the ferry.
I hug everyone one last time.

Good luck with the swim.

*Thanks, **Anthony**.*

Anthony!

Hey, Sammy, what're you doing here?

*I'm so cold, Anthony.
Please – do you have
more clothes?*

Let me see what I've got, he says.

I wait for him as he searches in the hut
and warm myself by a little electric heater.
My eyes are drawn to
a noticeboard on the wall.
It's full of photos.
Even one of me and Hamid
with Anthony.
I smile at the memory,
surprised that there are good ones
even in these circumstances.

Then my eyes are drawn to another.
The girl from the paper,
the girl who swims to help us.

Anthony comes back with
a hat, gloves, scarf and a big coat.
Will these do? he says.

This girl, Anthony,
when was she here?

Today actually.
She was volunteering.
She's swimming the Channel,
raising money for us.

Where is she now?

She just left.

I need to speak with her, Anthony.
I know her, I know her.

All right, mate,
calm down.
They were just outside so they
might not have left.

I run outside,
but the car isn't there.
I start to run down the hill
towards the motorway.

What about your clothes?
Anthony shouts,
but I can't answer.
I need to see her.

I'm running towards the motorway
as fast as my legs can carry me.
I'm like a crazy person,
looking at all the faces in the cars.
Everyone's **a blur**.

A blur. This whole day has gone by **so fast**.

So fast. The cars whizz **by**.

By the time we're on the motorway,
I've made up my mind that I'm
gonna **come back**.

Come back.
Please.
It's hopeless.
What was I even thinking?
I must be losing **my mind**.

My mind is racing
as **the traffic starts to slow down**.

The traffic starts to slow down
and **someone**

someone catches my eye,
a young boy –
I'm guessing my age.
He's so skinny,
skinnier than a boy of his age should be.
We catch each other's eyes
just for a second.

I can't believe it.
It's . . .

I can't believe it.
It's . . .

him . . .

her . . .

Our eyes meet.

Our eyes meet.

I'd never forget those eyes.

Her eyes are unforgettable.

I'm drawn to him and I don't know why.

I'm drawn to her and I don't know why.

It's as though I know him.

It's as though I know her.

I feel his pain.

I know her loss.

I know his loss.

I feel her pain.

And the traffic starts moving

And the traffic starts moving

        and we're

she's

        gone

gone.
I look behind

        and see him

her

    fade

       into

          the

             distance.

145 days before

A restless sleep.

          A restless sleep.

I see him.

          I see her

I can't breathe.

          The pain.

I'm drowning.

          I'm drowning.

So tired.

          So tired.

Is this the end?

          Is this the end?

A hand.

          A hand.

We meet.

          We meet.

His hand

          Her hand

in . . .

        mine

to-

        -gether

holding

        each other

looking into his eyes

        looking into her eyes

heart slowing

        heart racing

electricity

        through my bones

sinking

        sinking

            sinking

                sinking.

I	I
just	just
had	had
the	the
weirdest	weirdest
dream.	dream.

I open my email.
I take a photo of the boy
in the article being rescued in the sea.
I send it to the email address for
Care4Calais
with the hope

someone
will
know him.

Hi, Natalie here. I volunteered with my dad yesterday.
This is really weird, but do you recognize this boy?
I think I know him, and I'd like to get in touch.
Can you help?

I get a reply almost straight away.

Funny you should get in touch –
he said he knows you too.
How do you know each other?
Anthony
PS I don't think he has an email address, but he's
on FB **SammySJabir**.

144 days before

I haven't told anyone

        about the dream.

They'll think

        I'm losing my mind,

but the first time

        I saw him

her, in the

        paper,

I couldn't stop

        thinking about him

her.

        I've never experienced

anything like it before.

I wait for Anthony.
He always comes at 3 p.m.
with tea and biscuits,
and the Wi-Fi box and chargers.
I run to him
before he's even out of the van.

OK, take it easy.

Let me set everything up,
he says.

I read the article from the paper again.
YOU CAN FOLLOW NATALIE'S PROGRESS ON FACEBOOK.
I wait for my phone to charge.
There are twenty of us
gathered round,
watching,
waiting
for our phones to show life.

As soon as mine does,
I log into my account.
It shows I have a message.

I never have messages.

I open it.
I sit back in shock.

There's a message
from her.
From Natalie.

> Dear Sammy,
> It's so weird to message you,
> but we saw each other two days ago on the motorway
> and it felt really strange.
> Did you feel it too?
> This probably sounds totally random,
> but I just really felt the need to message you.
> Nat x

I show Hamid.
Oooh, he says, *British girlfriend.*

235

No, I say, it's nothing like that.
How should I reply?

Hamid looks over
my shoulder as I type.
Oh God, whatever you do,
don't write that!

Why not?

Because . . . you write creepy things.
'I had dream of you . . . have we met . . . ?'
She'll run a mile.

I press delete.

Go away, Hamid,
you're putting me off.

Tell her you need a visa, he says,
safe passage to the UK,
a home, education –
the list is endless.
You don't need a pen pal.

I ignore him and write

Dear Natalie,
It made me happy to see your message.
I think what you do to raise money for us is excellent.
Thank you.
I'm going to tell you something
and my friend Hamid told me not to put it.
But I have this feeling we know each other.
Can it be? Have you ever visited Eritrea?
I hope you message me back.
Sammy

A reply!
I start typing . . .

She's typing!

Hi Sammy,
You can tell your friend Hamid it's not strange.
I feel it too.
It's so weird.
I haven't told anyone.
They'd think I was losing my mind.
I've never been to Eritrea.
Where is it?
Soz my geography is crap.
Nat x

He's typing!

I type as fast as I can
before Anthony leaves
with the Wi-Fi box.

That's OK, not many people have heard of it.
It's a country in the Horn of Africa
bordered by Sudan and Ethiopia.
It's a beautiful country
but with many problems.

(I send a photo of the article.)

Look, your story makes it to France!

That's cool!
One last bit of weirdness.
Don't freak out,
but last night
I had a weird dream . . .

A dream where we were swimming . . .

Yes I had that dream.
Wait, this is freaky!

Totally!

What do you think it means?

Maybe we're connected?

How?

My mama says we all come from the same thing.
The same thing that made all the planets.
There is one thing that connects us all.

What?

Stardust.

Stardust?

143 days before

Tell me more about the stars, Sammy.

Everything that makes a star and the planets is in us.

So we're actually, literally, stardust?

Actually, literally, yes.

That's crazy.

We're so connected, it is crazy.
My baba would say, if people just realized that,
the world would be a better place.

That's for sure.

Baba once told me you have binary stars
that orbit each other from birth.
They're entwined.
Pulling towards each other.

What happens to them?

Eventually, they join.
Baba said that's what people are like.
We need one **another**.

142 days before

Rain pours down on our tent.
Hamid is sick,
coughing all night.
I pull the sleeping bag
over my head
to hide my tears.

.Hearing from Natalie
is the only thing
keeping me going.

Hiya, just me.
So, in answer to your question,
Dover's all right.
Where I live is a bit of a shithole,
but they're trying to make it better,
which means that now we can't really afford to live here.
It's like we're being pushed out.
Anyway, I don't wanna moan.
I know I'm really lucky in lots of ways.
I googled Eritrea.
I read an article saying it's like
the North Korea of Africa.
Sounds scary.

Messaging Sammy
is like
messaging
an old friend.
Someone I can confide in.
Someone who gets me
and I get them.

I spend the morning writing my reply.

> Mama and Baba were born
> into the thirty-year war for independence.
> Baba lost both his parents.
> He never got over it.
> Seven years later,
> two more years of war erupted with Ethiopia.
> It ended in 2000, and since then it's like
> the government is scared of another war.
>
> You have no choice but to go into the army
> at eighteen, sometimes younger.
> But it's not normal conscription,
> it's indefinite. It's slavery.
>
> That life was not for me.
> That is why we leave.

I give my phone to Anthony.
Have him check my spelling.
I don't want to look stupid.

All good, he says.
I press send.

I can't believe I never knew any of this, Mel.
It makes me feel sick.

How do you know he's telling the truth, Nat?

Because there are articles online that say the same thing.

It could be fake news.

What's wrong, Mel?

Nothing. I'm just saying.

This is gonna sound weird . . . but . . .

Spit it out, Nat . . .

It's like I know him. Like 'know' him 'know him' . . .
It's as if there's a connection.

Connection?

I told you, it's weird.

If you fancy him and you're having some sort of online affair, just say.

I don't fancy him – it's not like that.

How do you know he is who he says he is? Ever heard of grooming?

Cos I've seen him.

What? When?

On the way back from Calais. It was just for a second.

So you do fancy him?

No. Please believe me, there's no need to be jealous.

I can feel you drifting, Nat.

I'm not drifting. Just growing.
Isn't that what you **wanted**?

137 days before

Over the last week

we message

back

and

forth.

It's like a drug.

Personal stuff

(Mum, Dad, Ryan)

(Mama, Baba, Sophia, Tesfay)

and stupid stuff.

(Hilarious fail videos.)

(Cats being weird.)

I find myself staying up,

scrolling through all the messages,

reading every single one

again and

again.

135 days before

Hashim, a Sudanese man,
says he knows someone
who can buy us a boat.

We need three hundred euro, he says.
If I can get one hundred from each of you,
we can pool our money
and make the crossing.

I don't want to go on another boat, Hamid.
Never again.
I want to go by lorry, I say.

We can't be so narrow in our thinking, Sammy.
We have to take anything we can get.
Every night we try lorries.
Every night we're back here.
This could be our new hope.

I can't, Hamid. I can't.

Hamid looks disappointed.
When he's outside the tent with Hashim,
I hear him say that
he'll try to persuade me.

I switch on my phone
and read the last message from Natalie.

> Mum liked a sporting challenge,
> Lake Windermere, Channel relays,
> Great Lakes Swim, Great North Swim,
> you name it, she'd done it.
> A real-life mermaid.

No place she belonged more
than in the water.
She'd glide through it,
make it look effortless.
I've never seen anyone more at peace.
Cancer didn't stop her,
despite all the advice.
She was still determined to do the Channel swim.
'As long as I keep getting in, I'll get better.
You'll see, it's better than any chemo.'

I like hearing about your mother.
She sounds like a wonderful woman.

She really **was**.

132 days before

Tell me about your dad.

Baba was a civil servant but
he dreamed of becoming a professor of astronomy.
When I was little, I would sit in his lap
and he'd tell me all about the stars.

He was slender.
His hands were always warm.
His face was gentle.
He never raised his voice.

He used to say we lived in
difficult times,
dark times,
that when the time came
I would have to become a man
before I'd finished being a child.

We knew they were watching him.
Soldiers had come,
raided our belongings,
smashed our furniture,
and us.

The day it happened
I was hiding in the cellar.
I could only listen.

To hear a murder
is a strange thing.
From the cellar, it's difficult
to make out words.
Everything sounds like it's
underwater.

I heard furniture being moved
and feet stomping
as my parents hid anything
that might be deemed incriminating.
There was one second of silence
before the knock at the door.

It was a heavy knock.
A threatening knock.
A knock made with the sound of a
rifle against wood.
A knock I was used to hearing.
An unmistakable knock.

Knock
Knock
Knock.
Three knocks of death.

A scream.
A thud.
A prayer.

Gunshot.
Gunshot.
Gunshot.

Engine
screeching,
driving
away
into
the
             distance.

And then
silence.

Tell me about your mum.

Mum was my world.
She was a refugee support caseworker.
Spent her life caring for others.
She loved to sing
but couldn't.
Loved to run
but had dodgy knees.
So she found swimming.
It was like meditation, she said.
It was healing –
she needed it in her job.
She used to get depressed,
she thought she wasn't doing enough.
She wanted to change the world.

She had cancer.
It was a rare kind,
really aggressive.

I was there when she left us.
I was listening to her breathing,
and then she wasn't.

No hugs,
no speeches,
no goodbyes,
no nothing.

That's how people die, I guess.
They just
stop.

130 days before

I look forward to his messages.
Disappointed when a new one doesn't arrive,
excited when it lands.

> Great GIFs.
> Who doesn't like a kitten in a teacup!

Wish I could make you smile like that.

You do, Mel.

I stop scrolling through his messages,
put my arms round her
and kiss her, full on.
A kiss she won't forget.

Believe me now?

Dunno, she says.
I may need some more convincing.

And we fall back
on to her bed,
kissing,
touching,
skin on **skin**.

129 days before

I'm so exhausted from all my training.
I'm falling asleep
in front of the morning news
when I hear

CCTV footage of the racist attack
on Fazel Mahmood has been found.

I turn up the volume,
inch forward on the sofa
and watch the grey images
on the screen.

Three men in masks
kicking and punching Fazel,
who lies motionless on the ground.

I drop my bowl and
cornflakes soak into the carpet.
My heart is in my throat.
The image might be grainy,
but it's as clear as day to me.

The rose tattoo.
Ryan.

Ryan. Is. There.
Ryan is there,
kicking and punching.
Ryan is there,
kicking and punching
Fazel.

I can't stay silent,
not again.

I can't carry what he's done.

But he's your brother,
a voice inside my head says.
You don't snitch on family.

So
I wash the dishes.
I clean the carpet.
I sit on the sofa.
I watch the clip on YouTube.

Why you not at school, babe? You OK?

I ignore Mel's text.
I hold my phone,
finger frozen on send
for a text to Ryan.

I know what you did.

I delete.
I write it again.
I delete.
I watch the clip on YouTube.
I sit in my room.
I look out of the window.
I curl up in my duvet.
I watch the clip on YouTube.

Are you sick? Just message me back. Love you x

I ignore Mel's message.
I sit on the sofa.
I sit in the kitchen.
I sit on my bed.
The front door slams.
I walk downstairs.

Why aren't you at school, Nat?
I stand frozen.
What's happened, love?

I've lost my voice.
I give Dad my phone,
the web page already loaded.
I press play.
He doesn't need me to explain.
He sees what I see.

We're going to the police station, he says.
It's the right thing to do, Nat.
This can't go on.
Don't cry, Nat. **It's going to be OK,**
I promise.

It's going to be OK,
I promise, *Sammy*.

Fine, Hamid. I'll do it.

The last thing I want to do
is get on a boat,
but I have to admit
it is the only option
right now.

Thank you.
The sooner we can get the money
to Hashim . . .

. . . the sooner we get the boat.
Yes, I know how it works.

I close my eyes
and calm myself

by naming constellations.
Orion, Ursa Major,
Scorpius, Lyra,
Cygnus . . .
This has worked since I was a child.
Thinking of the stars makes me feel
connected to something
bigger than **me**.

Me.
Dad.
At the
police station.
The room
feels suffocating
and cold
and grey.
So grey.
Storm-cloud,
suffocating grey.

Do you think Ryan will ever forgive us, Dad?

I don't know, but we did the right thing, he says,
trying to convince himself that we **have**.

114 days before

I thought you said it would be a proper boat!
I say to Hashim.

This is a proper boat,
he says.

This skinny thing?
This is not a boat.

It's a kayak.
They're built to go fast.
You'll see once it has air inside it.

I can't believe it.
One hundred euros,
my share of this
stupid boat.

*What choice do I **have?***

***Have** you known for a long time?*
Fazel looks at me,
unblinking.
I want the truth.

The truth?
What is the truth?
I ask myself.
I can't look at him
because I have known
for a long time.
I just couldn't
admit it to myself.

The truth is I . . .
I suspected.

Fazel's mouth drops open
and he walks away from me.

Fazel, please!
Yes, I suspected,
but I didn't know for sure.
I had no proof.
I'm so sorry, Fazel.
Believe me,
I'm so sorry.

I was right about you all along.
I should have stuck with my first instincts.

What do you mean?

You always had another motive.
You were appeasing
your own guilt.
All this time . . .

No, that's not true . . .

Isn't it?

I watch him walk away.
Seeing the ugly truth
for the first time.

Maybe,
just maybe,
he's
right.

Right,
says Hashim,
I think that's it.

We prod the kayak.
It seems pretty solid.
It's taken all three of us
to blow it up.

Should we not have two oars,
like the picture on the box?
I ask.

Yes, but an extra oar was
another forty euro.
I'm told one is just as good.

I try not to panic.
Ursa Major, Ursa Minor,
Scorpius . . .

We wait till it's dark.
Only then do we push the kayak
off the beach and into the sea.
One by one we climb in.
Hashim is in the front,
Hamid in the middle,
I am at the back.

I look to the sky,
searching for the North Star.
But the clouds are thick tonight.

Hashim paddles,
guiding us towards
our new home.

Can you hear that? he asks.

That hissing sound?

The boat starts to
feel soft.
This can't be happening,
not again.

Hashim, Hamid!
We're sinking!
I scream.

The boat starts to deflate.

Get out and swim!
shouts Hashim.
Swim back to shore –
we can't be far.

The water is freezing.
Hamid, who can't swim,
panics and flaps
like a fish caught on a line.
Hashim grabs him
and swims.
I follow.
It's not long before our feet
touch the shore.
We drag ourselves out of the water
and lie down,
exhausted.

Hashim beats his fist
on the sand.

We **cry**.

110 days before

I'm just glad you're alive, Sammy.

I am never getting in another boat.

I wish I could do something to help.

Your messages give me hope.
Keep me going.
Tell me . . . how is it with your brother?
That was brave what you and your father did.

He's out on bail.
He's not staying with us – he's living with my nan.
We've not seen him or spoken to him since that night
we saw him in prison.
He's gonna plead guilty, he has to. The evidence is there.
Nan calls, tells us he's OK.
Dad looks like he's aged twenty years in the last
few weeks.
The only thing that takes our minds off him is training
for the swim.
It's the only time I see Dad look properly alive.
He keeps saying he's failed us.
I hear him on the phone to Nan.

Fazel won't talk to me.
I don't blame him.

I'm a coward.
He's right about me.
I'm fucking horrible.
I'm the worst.

Sorry, I don't mean to feel sorry for myself.
I'm embarrassed that I'm moaning to you.

Don't say these things, Natalie.
I understand that you may feel hopeless right now.
My baba used to say that even in the dark stars still shine,
so keep looking up, Natalie.
It will get better.

I hope you make it over here soon.

Me **too**.

103 days before

Is everything OK?
I haven't heard from you in a while.
I woke up this morning and realized it's just over
three months till my swim.
I swam in the sea this morning –
it's so much better than training in a pool.
We've raised nearly four thousand pounds.
I can't believe it.
I hope you're OK?
Nat

Natalie,
I'm sorry I haven't written for so long.
Things here are really bad.
The police spray our tents
they burn our shelter
they beat us.
Anything they can to
break us down.

I watched a video of
police kicking and punching refugees
on YouTube.
The comments made me sick,
'Scum, good on the police'
'No one wants them here – tell them to go back'
'Black bastards'.

Honestly, Natalie,
I feel like I can't go on for much longer.
No hope, no love, no future, no nothing.
Sammy

Sammy,
Please don't say those things.
Remember what your dad used to say –
there are stars in the dark, right?
Keep looking up, Sammy.
There is hope, I promise.
Please message me back.
Let me know you're OK.
Nat xxx

102 days before

The police attack us at night.
Catch us as we try to sleep.
Round us up like cattle.
Hamid and I are taken to
a processing centre.

We're only ten minutes in the coach.
I had no idea a prison was so close.
Memories of the centre in Turin
come flooding back.
My heart beats fast
and my legs go weak
as I picture another
barbed-wire cage.

We are told we're
illegal migrants.
Baba used to say,

> *Everyone is on the move,*
> *always has been,*
> *always will.*

What makes it OK?
The colour of your skin?
There are British
who live in Europe.
They are called expats,
not immigrants.
Language can so easily
put you on top
if you're lucky enough
to be the ones
giving out the labels.

I guess migration is only
a human right
if you're the
right type of **human**.

98 days before

No messages from Sammy for five days.
He's not even reading the ones I've sent.
No blue ticks.

I email Anthony.
I haven't heard from Sammy in a while.
Is he **OK**?

OK. *Which country have you come from?*
> *Eritrea.*
What's the capital?
> *Asmara.*
How much does a loaf of bread cost in Eritrea?
> *About seventy-five nakfa.*
How much is a bag of rice?
> *Maybe thirty nakfa.*
How much is a litre of milk?
> *Erm . . . twenty nakfa, twenty-five maybe.*
Which number bus do you take to the airport from Asmara?
> *Service number 1.*

These are the questions they ask
to determine
whether I can
be given asylum status.
I shake as I answer each one.

Eritrea is not listed as a dangerous country.

It is, I say, *dangerous, I mean.*

But
it's no good.
No matter what I say,

I'm not believed.
Because,
according to these people,
Eritrea,
the country that enforces
military conscription
and a lifetime of
slave labour,
the country that has
shut itself off
from the rest of the world
so it can imprison
and torture
its population without trial,
the country that does not allow
free speech,
is not
a
dangerous
country.

97 days before

Hi Natalie,
The police rounded up everyone in the camp south of
the nature reserve a few nights ago.
They've been taken to various centres around Calais
and Paris. I'm trying to find out where Sammy is.
Anthony

When the stars come out,
I look to them for answers,
for hope.

When the stars come out,
I look to them for answers,
for hope.

But I am fading.
Becoming a ghost.
In detention
no one knows
when they're
going to leave.

The waiting
is the **worst**.

78 days before

Ryan's date in court
is in six weeks' time.

In six weeks' time
my brother
will be sentenced
to **prison**.

Prison would be better
than this place.
In prison there's an
end date.
Detention
is a vicious,
never-ending cycle.
No clean clothes
no right-fitting shoes
no home that's our own
no security
no love
no belonging
no hopes
no dreams.

Self-harm
hunger strikes
suicide
overcrowding
slowly losing our minds in
nightmares and panic attacks.

Nightmares and panic attacks –
that's what it's been like for me, Natalie.

Do you have any idea?

I'm sorry, Fazel,
I didn't know.
I jus–
I just . . . want to let you know that
I'm here for you.
I know I'm the last person you want to see,
but I am . . .
I'd do anything
to be mates again.

I need to be alone.

I watch Fazel walk away and
fall into Mel's arms.

You're gonna have to give him time, Nat.

I'm losing everyone, **I cry**.

I cry
every night.
People become
different
in this **place**.

65 days before

I got an email from Anthony
a few days ago.

We're having a demonstration outside the detention
centre where Sammy is being held.
Do you want to join us?

Dad and I drive to Calais again.
We meet Anthony outside the detention centre –
a horrible-looking place
surrounded by barbed wire.
It looks like a prison.

I managed to speak to him a few days ago.
He sounded bad.
Waiting to hear about his asylum application.
I told him you send love and that you've been thinking of him.
He seemed to cheer up a bit after that.

We stand outside the centre
with big hearts and banners that say
WE'RE SORRY.
YOU MATTER.
YOU ARE LOVED.

I have a bunch of purple
heart-shaped balloons
floating from my wrist.
I wish they would carry me over,
so I could rescue everyone in there.

We wave when we see people.
A crowd has gathered in the yard
and they wave back.
I hope Sammy is **there**.

There are people demonstrating
outside the centre.
Wave back, I say to Hamid,
who stands with his hands
in his pockets,
looking at the ground.

What's the point? he says.

It shows there's still love, Hamid.

My eyes fix on purple heart-shaped balloons
floating and bouncing in the air.

Am I worthy?
Do I love?
Do I feel?

Yes.
Yes, I **do**.

5 days before

The last 60 days:

I ask about my asylum application.
How much longer? No answer.
Hamid no longer speaks,
a fight breaks out in the canteen and
we have a new cellmate from Iraq, Zamir.
He speaks no English.
All we do is smile at each other.
They do not change the food
in this place.
The same gruel for
seven days.

Seven days,
nine hours
and forty-five minutes.
That's how long I have
until my six-hour
qualifying swim in Dover harbour.
It's getting close.
My nerves sometimes get the better of me.

Every weekend from now until my date
is spent down at the harbour training with
other Channel swimmers who gather at the beach every
Saturday and Sunday.
I look at Dad.
Do you think I've got what it takes? **I ask**.

I ask about my asylum application.
How much longer? No answer.
I am always hungry.

New cellmate Zamir seems very sad.
I wish we could communicate.
I wonder if Natalie knows where I am.
Last night I couldn't sleep.
Zamir has nightmares.
Hamid sinks into a dark place.
I am worried.

I am worried.
I'd be lying if I said I wasn't.
This is the real test.
The six-hour qualifier.
There's a big part of me that doesn't feel ready.
I should have taken the date in August next year.

Remember, Nat: it's mind over matter out there.
You've got the fitness, you've done the training.
There's no reason why you can't do this.

OK, Dad.

That's my girl.

My body trembles with nerves,
my stomach somersaults.

First hour, I'm strong.
Second hour, I'm feeling it.
Third hour, it's tough.
Shoulders aching.
Fourth hour, it's gruelling and
my body is numb.
Fifth hour, I feel sick.
I think my organs might shut down.

Mind over matter, Nat.
Keep going.
One arm

over the other,
one kick at a time.

Final hour, my skin burns.
I can only think of the next stroke,
the next breath.
One two breathe.
One two breathe.

My legs are jelly.
I stumble out of the sea.
Dad gives me a hug and
I collapse on the sand,
bursting into tears.

Nat, what's wrong?
Mel puts her arms round me.

It's happy tears.
I think it's all just hit me.
I'm gonna do this, aren't I?
I'm actually gonna swim the Channel!

Yes you are, Nat.
Dad shows me his time sheet.
And if you keep up that pace,
*you're looking at a decent **time**!*

Time passes.
I ask about my asylum application.
How much longer? No answer.
I try making Hamid laugh.
It doesn't work.
The food in this place never changes.
I watch TV.
Only one channel is working,
and I don't understand French.
I get a phone call from Anthony.

It makes me feel better all **day**.

Daylight streams through
the stained-glass windows
in the courtroom.
I see Fazel, who sits with his foster family and Mel.
Ryan stands with two police officers, one each side of him.

How do you plead?

Guilty,
he says quietly.
It's the only time
Ryan looks up.
It's the first time Dad and I have seen him
since he was bailed.
He looks thin,
and pale.
Half the man he used to be.

Ryan Sebastian Lennon,
you are charged with racially aggravated grievous bodily harm,
criminal damage and violent disorder . . .
three years six months . . .

Ryan loses the muscles in his legs,
and buckles.
Two police officers hold him up.
He looks at Dad, at me,
tears running down his face.

It had to be done, whispers Dad.
It had to be done.

When can we see him? **I ask**.

I ask about my asylum application.
How much longer? No answer.
Zamir hears back about his asylum application.
Denied.
Hamid has become mute.
Talk to me, I say.
Talk to me.

Talk to me*, Fazel.*
Please.
Is there any way we can be
mates again?

Maybe. I spoke with my foster parents –
they helped me to see.

I know nothing I say will ever make it right.

My foster mother, she says
it's not your crime.
I'd like it if we could move forward.
I hate to admit it,
but I miss your friendship.

I want that more than anything, Fazel.
Don't suppose I can get a hug?

Sure.

> *Oi oi, refugee lover got herself a refugee fuck boy.*
> *Ain't your girlfriend gonna get jealous?*

Kevin!
I shout, walking towards him,
backing him into a corner.

You're a sad piece of shit, you know that?

Before he has the chance for a comeback,
I kick him between the legs.
He slides down the wall,
holding his crotch,
tears streaming down **his face**.

His face
empty,
no life behind his eyes.
We try to get him out of bed, but
Zamir doesn't want to
join us for breakfast.

When we arrive back at the cell,
I see feet floating in mid-air.
Hamid covers my eyes
and drags me out of the cell.
Help! he shouts. *Help!*
We hold each other,
my body shaking.

My body shaking,
standing in front
of the whole school.

Mrs Edwards has called me up
to stand next to her in assembly.
She announces my swim is in under two weeks.
I'm asked if I want to say a few words.
I shake my head,
my cheeks beetroot red.
Mel takes my place.
Thanks everyone on my behalf and
reveals that we've reached our target.
Everyone applauds.
Mel beams with delight.
my legs feel like they might
give way.

You may well be coming back to school in September as a
Channel swimmer, Natalie!
Mrs Edwards announces to the school.

There's nothing more I can do.
This. Is. **It**.

It frightens us to sleep in our cell,
so Hamid and I sleep in the corridor.
I realize I haven't seen starlight
in nearly two **months**.

ZAMIR RAJA

22.6.2001 – 10.7.2019

4 days before

My asylum claim
has been rejected.

I told the truth.
But still they get ready
to send me back.

Back to hell
through hell.

When I sleep,
I have a nightmare.

> The room
> fills with water
> and I
> fight and fight and fight
> until I can no longer fight
> and I sink
> and sink
> and sink.

I wake,
wishing I'd gone the way Tesfay did,
wishing I had the guts to do what Zamir did.
Anything to end this pain.

I sit in the corner
of my cell.
**Unable to move,
finding it hard
to breathe.**

Unable to move,
finding it hard
to breathe,
looking at Dad,
Dad looking at Ryan,
Ryan looking at his feet.

Why'd you do it, son?

He shrugs.

You would have got a shorter sentence
if you'd just given them the names
of the others.

Ryan looks at the floor.

And where are they now, eh?
Have they been to visit?
This Danny fella,
have you heard from him?

Ryan looks at the wall.

No, I didn't think so.
They don't give a shit about you, Ryan.

Ryan drops his face
into his hands.
His whole body shakes.

You're sorry though, aren't you, son?

Everything felt so shit and . . .
and . . . I dunno,
it just made me feel like I mattered . . .

And now? How'd you feel now?
You know you did wrong, don't you?

I just need to hear you say it, Ryan . . .

I've been so stupid, Dad.
What have I done?
*What have I **done**?*

3 days before

I escape
in the night.

Hamid. We have to go. They'll send us back.
Come with me.

I'm still waiting to hear about my asylum claim.
I might be lucky.

See you in the UK one way or another, Hamid.

Good luck, Sammy.

I make a break for it over the fence.
The beach is close,
no more than a twenty-minute walk.
I rush through streets
I don't know
in the dark.

This twenty-minute walk
takes hours
as I go in circles
and lose my way in the night.

I stand on the motorway.
        I stand looking at the sea.
I stand on the motorway.
        I stand looking at the sea.

There's no way to know
which is the right way.

How many lives do I get?
I didn't die in the Sahara.

I didn't die in the Mediterranean.
I didn't die in the Channel,
but do I get a second chance?
I hear Tesfay.

The chance to live is worth dying for.

2 days before

I see Anthony.
He hugs me and
gives me a plate of food.

I cry and cry,
tell him
how my application
failed.
The torture.
Zamir.

He tells me   he cannot imagine my pain.
He tells me   he is sorry.
He tells me   he wishes he could make it right.
He tells me   Natalie has kept in touch.

I tell him I saw the demonstration.
He tells me she was there.

Before he leaves with the Wi-Fi,
I send Natalie a message.

> I'm back.
> Sorry for the long silence.
> Tell me your news.
> Sammy

> Sammy!! How are you???
> Have you heard about your asylum application yet?
> Anthony emailed and said you should know soon.
> I'm keeping all my fingers and toes crossed!
>
> Well, I have a full twenty-four hours of good conditions.
> EEEEK, I can't believe it.

I'll be starting at 10 p.m. from Samphire Hoe in Dover.
I don't think I could have done this without you.
I need you to know that. Thank you.
I've raised over £4,000. Can you believe it?
Nat xxx

Natalie, I wish you all the luck in the world.
You've also been a great friend over the last few months.
Thank YOU. I write this from the bottom of my heart.
I also have good news.
My asylum application was a success!
I cannot believe it. I'm in shock.
I hope this good news gives you
an extra burst of energy
to complete your big swim.
Sammy x

PS Tonight, Natalie, look at the stars.
I will be looking too.
They are the same ones you see.
This is how we are all connected.
It seems silly for people to think
we are so different.
We are not.
We came from them.
We're all built from the same **dust**.

1 day before

I sit at Mum's grave.

Tomorrow's the big day, Mum.
I'm wearing your swimming costume and cap.
That way a little bit of you will make it across too.
I'm doing it, Mum.
I'm finishing what you started.
Wish me luck.
*This is **it**.*

It is the same as before.
I wait at the motorway
all night.
No luck.

I hear Hamid.
You can't keep doing the same thing.
I stare out at the sea.
I throw stones,
see how far
I can make them skim
along the surface.

The sea is calm,
like glass,
and I wish I could
walk straight over it,
all the way to paradise.

I call Mama.
I made it, I say.
I made it to the UK.
She cries.
Tears of joy, she says.

I sit on the beach,
feeling strangely calm.
I look at the water.
I will try something different
and, if I die,
that's **OK**.

0 days before

Almost a year of training.
This is it, Natalie. Whatever happens today,
you did it. You've done all the hard work.

I couldn't have done it without you, Dad.

I couldn't have come through this year without you, Natty.
You've really pulled me through.
Your mum would be so proud.
Now go and swim the Channel, my girl.

He puts the last of the grease on my face
and I jump off the boat and swim towards the shore.
My mind goes to Sammy.
I'm so happy he's safe.
It's given me the boost I need
to start this marathon swim.
I look up at the stars,
imagine Sammy looking up too.
This is for you, I whisper.

When I step on to the beach,
there's a big crowd gathered,
with banners and balloons.
It looks like half the school has turned up,
but I can only focus on Mel and Fazel.

I wish I could hug you both, but I'm covered in grease.

We're going to stay awake till you finish.
I believe in you, she says.

Fazel takes a picture.
One now and one after. You can do this!

289

Love you, guys. Thank you!
I shout to all the supporters.

Dad waves from the boat.
I wave back.
The horn blows
and **I step into the water**.

I step into the water.
My breath catches mid-gasp
I'm unable to breathe it back in.
I stand choked,
willing it back into **my body**.

My body glides through
the water
one stroke at a time,
one breath at a time.

One breath at a time.
I step deeper and deeper
into the water,
the ice-cold water.
I fight the urge to go back.

I go deeper.
Water covers
my ankles,
then my shins.
Water sloshes round my knees,
stones fall away beneath my feet,
I'm in up to my waist.

I dip my head under,
my feet no longer touching earth.

I'm swimming.
I laugh.
A wave comes right over my head.
I kick my legs,
I swing my arms,
I swim in the ink-black sea.

I stretch one arm over,
then the other.
I kick my legs.
I lift my head to the side.
I take a breath.

One two three four
breathe.
One two three four
breathe.

I am here –
it's a miracle.
It's a miracle I'm still alive.
What was the point of everything before
if I'm to fall at the last hurdle?
I must make it.
I will make it.

I will make it.
I have to make it.
One stroke after the next.
I don't know how long I've been going.
I don't want to ask.
It's still dark.

It's still dark.
Am I halfway?
The waves are getting bigger.

I struggle to swim.
Cold and tired.
I can see the lights of tankers.

I have no idea where I'm swimming,
how far I have to go,
how far I have come,
how long I have been in the water.
**I feel sick,
I'm so cold.**

    **I feel sick,
    I'm so cold.**

But I keep going.

    Keep going.

I must keep going.

    Keep going.

I feel like I'm

    fading.

I feel like I'm

    disappearing.

I see Mum . . . *Keep going, Nat.*
Mum?

I see Baba ... *My stargazer!*
Baba?

I reach out to her.

I reach out to him.

She's gone.

He's gone.

Mum?

Baba?

Where
did
you
go?

I am exhausted.

I can't go on.

Night becomes day.

I see a figure in the water.

           I see a figure in the water.
           Sammy?

Nat?

           Hallucinations, Nat.

Nat?

           Sammy?

Is this real?

           His hand

her hand

           in . . .

mine

to–

           –gether

           holding

each other

looking into his eyes

looking into her eyes.

He is gone.

She is gone.
Natalie?

Sammy?

Where . . .

are you?

I'm so exhausted.
My mind playing tricks.
Hallucinations, Nat.
You didn't see Mum.
You didn't see Sammy.

Is my mind playing tricks?
I look around me.
Natalie?
Natalie?
There's no one.
Nothing.
Just ink-black sea
with the North Star as my guide.

If you are lost or you need guidance,
just look up,
see this star
and it will lead you towards hope.

There's nothing like sunrise.

The darkness seems never-ending.
I swim
I swim
I swim.
It feels like forever.
Will I ever finish?
So cold.
Don't freeze, Sammy,
don't freeze.
I hear Baba.
Fight, Sammy.
Fight.

Fight, Nat.
Fight.
The last stretch.
I can see the beach.
I can see it!
Fifteen hours later.
I hear cheering
as **my feet touch sand**.

My feet touch sand.
Thank you, God.
I kiss the sand.
Thank you, God.
I inhale the earth and
cough and cough and cough.

I lie on my back.
Looking up at the stars.

I made it.
I made it.
I made it.

5 days after

No word from Sammy.
Five days.
Nothing.

How long have I
been asleep?
Is it day or night?
It's hard to tell.
I see two figures in the distance.

Hey!
They can't hear.

Hey!
They can't hear.
My throat burns.

Hey!
They can't hear.
My muscles snap
as I try to get to my feet.

Hey!
They can't hear.
I stumble, crawl,
pull myself towards them.
These two shadowy figures.

Hey!
They can't hear.
They pull a fishing net
out of the water.

Hey!
They can't hear.
I pull myself closer.
They pull the net harder.

Hey!
They can't hear.
I'm close,
touching the man's hands.

Hey!
They can't hear.
They inspect their net.

Hey!
They can't hear.
I stand in front of them.

Oh God, says a man.
Oh God, says the other.

Hey!
They can't hear.
One man is sick in the sand.

Hey, I need food, water. Please help me.
They can't hear.
The vomiting man cries.
The other fumbles with his phone.

Hey! I shout. *Why aren't you listening?*

I fall to the floor.
I look into the net.
A body.
A face.

My
body.
My
face.

My body.
My face.
In the net
staring back at me.

The man is sick again.
The other man says,
Police and ambulance.

I look down at myself.
Stretch out my hand **to** . . .

6 days after

There's a message going round on social media.
Graphic content.
I can't help but click.
You know you shouldn't,
but the danger of it,
the danger
of what you might see,
pulls you in.

It takes a while to load,
but when it does . . .
I lose control.
Fall to the floor and weep.

His eyes are closed,
but I know it's him.
I know it's **Sammy**.

7 days after

At the coroner's.
I confirm
it's **him**.

SAMUEL SALIH JABIR

11.3.2000 – 21.7.2019

8 days after

Dear Anthony,
I don't know if you've heard, but Sammy died. He
drowned. I don't understand how this happened. Why
would he try and swim all the way? He'd been given
asylum.
Nat

Dear Nat,
His asylum claim had been rejected. That's why he was
back at the camp. He escaped from the centre. I blame
myself. I should have noticed something. I should
have known how hopeless he was feeling. I could have
stopped him. Please let me know when the funeral is.
I'd like to come.
Anthony

9 days after

What did I miss?
I re-read every message,
looking for clues.

What did I miss?
It must be here between the lines,
the spaces between his words.

What did I **miss**?

12 days after

A knock at the door.

Can you get it, Mel?

She peels herself away from me
only to return a moment later.

It's Fazel, and he's brought someone to see you.
I think you're gonna want to meet them.

I slowly unravel myself.

Hi, I croak.
Looking at Fazel and then the stranger
standing opposite me.
His eyes are swollen.
It looks like he's been crying too.

My name is Hamid.
Sammy was my friend.
More than just a friend.
Brother.

Hamid. Yes, he wrote about you.

Yes?

His eyes light up
and
we let ourselves
fall into each **other**.

13 days after

Hello?

My name is Hamid. I knew Sammy – we travelled together.

Yes.

Is this Helen?

No, Sophia.

Sophia? Sammy's sister? He said you were in Sawa.

I escaped. I'm hiding, for now . . .
Why are you calling? Where is Sammy?

I hear him say the words, shaking as he speaks.

I feel her chest cave with the weight of a thousand rocks.
I feel her heart shatter into a million pieces.

Sophia . . . He talked about all of you every day.
So many stories. You were always in his thoughts . . .

Pain accompanies every word.
I can't believe it. Sammy's gone.
We hear his mum crying.
We hear her scream his name,
Sammy Sammy Sammy.

I'm so sorry.

There are long silences
as they try to find the right words.

Hamid, when you take his ashes,
you put them somewhere special,
somewhere that will carry him
to the stars.
Promise me.

I promise.

22 days after

We stand on top of the white cliffs,
a group of us, some known –
Anthony, Hamid, Fazel, Mel –
but mostly people who have heard,
people who want to pay their respects.

Hamid holds a piece of paper,
shaking as he speaks.
I have some words from his mother and sister Sophia.
When Sammy was a small boy,
he learned all the constellations by heart.
You could point to the sky and he could tell you
which stars they were.
This is how smart he was.
He feared all insects, especially spiders,
yet he never killed a single one.
This is how kind and gentle he was.
Despite how scared he was to leave,
he knew it was what he had to do
if he was to have a chance to live freely.
This is how brave he was.
So please don't forget him,
for he is like thousands who have gone before.
Please don't forget him.
His journey is like that of a million more.

We scatter his ashes.
I imagine them being carried
up into the sky,
landing among the **stars**.

366 days after

Rain pelts down
on the metal roof
of our makeshift kitchen.
A queue of hungry people
has formed, waiting eagerly
for their one hot meal.

Nothing has changed in Calais
since the last time I was here:
camps are dismantled
tents destroyed
belongings burned
people handcuffed
driven away
before more desperate
humans arrive.

I've found my way back
one day at a time,
trying to do better.
Through all the heartbreak,
the ugly,
and the loss of the last year,
I never stop looking up.

Natalie, look at the stars.
I will be looking too.
They are the same ones you see.
This is how we are all connected.
It seems silly for people to think
we are so different.
We are not.
We came from them.
We're all built from the same ***dust***.

Author's note

The story you have read is a work of fiction. Unfortunately, elements of Sammy's journey are not. Every year millions of men, women and children flee war, conflict, violence, persecution or, in Sammy's case, indefinite military service and human rights abuses, and thousands die each year trying to make the journey.

In 2018 I ran two community arts projects, working with women from all walks of life, many of whom had refugee status. The projects focused on fictional storytelling, but it soon became clear that the participants wanted to talk about and share their experiences with each other and most importantly they wanted their personal stories to be heard by others.

These projects coincided with a year of far-right demonstrations around the UK with protests 'attracting biggest numbers since 1930s', according to research from the Commission for Countering Extremism. These protests had an effect on everyone in the group. 'They are protesting people like me. I come here for safety; I am not a threat,' said a participant who had not long arrived in the UK.

I felt compelled to shed light on both these issues, especially as I myself had recently moved to a coastal town where the arrival of refugees by boat was a daily occurrence, leading to increasing tensions within the town. Despite these divisions, I wanted to remind people of how connected we all are. *The Crossing* is about loss, but it is also about hope and wanting more than anything to belong and feel safe. Isn't that all anyone wants? Isn't that what everyone deserves?

Acknowledgements

A lot of research went into the writing of this book. I spoke with people who had themselves experienced the same horrors and made the same journey as Sammy had taken. I want to say thank you for sharing and trusting me with your stories.

I will forever be grateful to Aida Silvestri, who works tirelessly helping Eritrean refugees through multiple charities. Thank you for guiding me through this novel and ensuring its integrity and honesty. Thank you to Sandy and Sadie for reading the manuscript when I was panicked and offering invaluable advice and guidance.

Thank you to Annie for sharing your Channel swimming tips, tricks and training plans! And to Malcom who first spoke with me about Channel swimming and convinced me to start sea swimming.

Thank you to my agent Felicity and the entire team at Penguin. In particular, my editors Carmen and Millie, managing editors Wendy and Shreeta, copy-editor Jane, proofreaders Sarah and Anthony, designers Janene and Emily, and finally David Foldvari for his cover art.

The final shout-out has to go to my very own moon and stars, Joe. I don't know where I'd be without you. I certainly wouldn't be writing. xxx